Enemy by Association
By: D. C. Shaftoe

Praise for D. C. Shaftoe

"**D. C. Shaftoe** has written a compelling spy story and romance...this is an excellent novel and I look forward to more from this author...highly recommended."

- Elaine Fuhr of *AllBooks Review* on
Forged in the Jungles of Burma

"This book starts off with a bang-up car crash and continues its pace at the same speed, never letting up on the proverbial gas...**Shaftoe** does a wonderful job of balancing the plot's action with Brock's real and endearing concern for his wife...she uses just the right amount of humor in her writing which helps to make all of her characters very real...a sophisticated spy who has a heart pounding adventure...packed with plenty of action, this book delivers what readers want."

- Wendy Thomas of *AllBooks Review* on
Assassin's Trap

Books by D. C. Shaftoe

Forged in the Jungles of Burma

Assassin's Trap

Enemy by Association
Copyright © 2012 D. C. Shaftoe

ISBN: 978-0-9684127-5-6

www.dcshaftoe.com

Dedication

To my children, Nathanael and Jared, I'm your biggest fan.

To my nieces and nephews (in alphabetical order, just to be fair), Danille, David, Joshua, Natalie, Sade, Tyrone, Vanessa

Delight yourself in the Lord and He will give you the desires of your heart.   Psalm 37:4

Contents

CHAPTER 1

Chaos shattered the stillness. The tranquility which Ethan Lange had sought amongst the works of art in Washington's National Gallery could not abide in the reality of seven gunmen loaded for bear with AK-47s and smoke grenades. Taking in the scene in a snapshot of time, Ethan watched the young and the old, the singles, the groups, and even the security guards run for cover at the staccato of gunfire tracing an arc around the Rotunda of the main foyer.

Everyone ran. Everyone except the young mother and her two little boys, one clinging tightly to her neck and the other huddled, whimpering on the floor. Reacting without thought, Ethan strode toward the little family and pulled the cringing boy up into his grip, covering his scream with a large hand. The boy froze in his arms.

Ethan forestalled the mother's protest with a terse, "Quiet! Follow me."

Immediately sprinting away, Ethan aimed for the stairs to the 7th Street entrance. The rhythm of her footsteps assured him that the mother followed. Turning right at the bottom, away from the café and gift shop which were teeming with screaming tourists, Ethan led his little parade toward the largest marble sculpture in the Special Collections room. Firmly gripping the mother's arm, he shoved her and the younger blonde-haired boy between the enormous carving and the wall. He then handed in the older, sandy-haired boy. Pulling out his cell phone, Ethan crouched protectively at the entrance to the space.

"Fire, ambulance or police?"

"Police," Ethan said.

"What is the nature of your emergency?"

"Gunfire at the National Gallery," he said.

"Is anybody hurt?"

"I don't know. Transfer me to the agent in charge. Clearance code 99672," Ethan said and waited through an interminable silence for the operator's response.

"I'm sorry, sir, that code doesn't work. But I need you to stay calm—"

Frustration surging through his chest, Ethan replied, "I am perfectly calm. Transfer me to the Armed Response Unit immediately."

"Sir, there's no need to use that tone—"

Ethan snapped his phone shut and muttered bitterly, "One mistake and I'm cut off."

Tapping urgently on his back, the mother asked in a shaky whisper, "Who are you? What's happening?"

"Agen—" Ethan paused. He wasn't an FBI agent any longer, probably never would be again. "Ethan Lange," he said, keeping his voice quiet, not in the least interested in drawing unwanted attention. "There are several gunmen upstairs. Stay quiet."

Ethan heard the confused voices of the little boys.

"Mommy, what's wrong?"

"I'm scared."

The drum of footsteps approached. Looking back over his shoulder, Ethan said, "Keep them quiet," and then asked, "What's your name?" People always responded more quickly to orders if you could call them by name.

"Sarah. Sarah Maier," she said.

"Sarah, I'm going to find out what's going on and see what I can do. Keep them quiet," Ethan said.

Sarah nodded, pulling the boys more tightly to her in the confined space.

Using the exhibits as cover, Ethan inched his way into the hall while he tried to gain a perspective on his next move. Tourists huddled together in the gift shop. *Why do they stand there waiting to be terrorized? The exit is ten feet away!* Ethan started toward them but stopped when two gunmen appeared, firing over the heads of the crowd in a staccato of intimidation.

"Be still and be silent!" roared one man, his heavy lisp taking some of the fierceness from his orders. Another volley of gunfire replaced it. "Walk upstairs in an orderly fashion. Go!"

Ethan slipped back along the hallway. At the telltale sound of booted feet approaching, he ducked into a small exhibit room filled with scrolls and parchments.

"Have you located him?" The voice was vaguely familiar, the accent was Russian, or more likely, Chechen.

"Not yet, sir," replied another man in a rumbling voice with a thick southern accent, reminding Ethan of Foghorn Leghorn. Except good ole Foghorn didn't carry an AK-47. Not in the cartoons that Ethan had watched anyway.

"If he is not with the tourists in the gift store, then he must be in this vicinity. Continue searching," the Chechen replied, his steps retreating down the hallway toward the Special Collections room. And Sarah.

Uncharacteristically, a jolt of panic lit in Ethan's chest. Something about Sarah pulled at Ethan's conscience, at his heart. Clearly, sometime in the past six minutes, Ethan had lost his objectivity. His need to rescue Sarah and the little boys drove him back, skirting in and around the exhibits and through the connecting doorways to the Special Collections room. Squatting back against the wall, he quick-checked the corner to see the gunmen examining each nook and cranny that could hold a body. What to do to save Sarah and her little boys?

Darting into the room across the hall, Ethan grabbed a vase—not Ming, *I hope*—and tossed it across the hallway to shatter against the doorjamb of the Special Collections room. Movement ceased for a moment across the hall, followed by the jabber of consternation. Seconds later, footsteps moved in his direction. When a head appeared in the doorway, Ethan chopped down, stunning the gunman and deftly removing the man's rifle. Another punch to the head knocked him out cold.

Ethan checked the ammunition in the clip and dragged the unconscious gunman out of the doorway, gagging him with his own neckerchief and binding his wrists.

"Miguel!" Ethan heard the southern drawl again. "Miguel!"

*Miguel's out of commission, dude. And if you'll just come a little closer...*Mumbling an unintelligible reply, Ethan lured the second gunman closer until he emerged within the room. This man, however, was not so easily dispatched. He was taller, stronger, all bulk and intimidation.

Freezing at the click of Ethan cocking Miguel's rifle, Foghorn slowly raised his hands as he turned to face Ethan. Without warning, Foghorn struck out, forcing Ethan to retreat to avoid the onslaught of blows, blows which came from fists that were more like sledge hammers than flesh and bone.

"He—" Foghorn began to call out. Clasping his fists together and aiming for Foghorn's vulnerable throat, Ethan punched out to silence the cry for support. The movement cost him, leaving an opening which Foghorn immediately used to his advantage, connecting with Ethan's solar plexus. Ethan dropped like a stone to the floor, fighting the spasm which stole his breath.

Kicking out weakly, Ethan tried to move away, fighting to keep Foghorn from once again connecting. Finally drawing a shuddering breath, Ethan rolled away, over bits of pottery, staggering into a crouch with no idea as to where Miguel's rifle had disappeared.

"Cease!" the Chechen said. His voice rang with command.

Ethan was grateful for the reprieve.

"Mr. Lange, isn't it?" The Chechen seemed only mildly curious. "Are you alone?"

Ethan straightened to address the man, and was immediately immobilized by the combination of meaty hands and the muzzles of two AK-47s thrust into his face. A rifle butt slammed into his knee and Ethan stumbled, biting back a moan.

Looking up, Ethan had his first glimpse of the man behind his current troubles, Borz Vakh, Chechen rebel turned international gun-for-hire. Vakh stood as a conundrum in the world of international politics. He claimed to be the cast-off son of a cast-off descendent of the Russian czar, Nicholas himself. But rather than uniting his cause to Chechnya's oppressors, instead, it set him against it. The crisis of identity had created a man who fancied himself cultured and noble, a cut above the rest; a man who had detached from any fabric of connectedness, peddling his skills on the common market, a man with no allegiance, a noble with no nobility.

Vakh stood straight and tall, his black curls carefully coiffed and his moustache trimmed. The silken khaki fatigues he wore gave him a military appearance with an effete air.

Vakh struck out, a blow as fast as lightning, to slap Ethan for his tardiness in responding.

"Ah, Mr. Lange, I repeat. Are you alone?" Vakh said, drawing out his words.

Clenching his jaw to hold back the words he *wanted* to say, Ethan replied, "I'm alone."

"Your wife and children?" Vakh asked.

"What do you mean?" Ethan's gaze jerked to the man's face.

"The security cameras clearly showed you with a woman and two children," Vakh said.

He'd merely asked Sarah a question, before the chaos began, but Vakh must have been monitoring the closed circuit security and come to believe that they were together. *I need to make Vakh believe that Sarah and the little boys are gone so he won't look for them.* Thinking furiously, Ethan replied, "My wife took them to get a head start on the Washington Zoo."

Vakh began to turn away and then paused, turning back as he clapped his hands behind his back, a thoughtful expression on his face. "I'm not certain I believe you, Mr. Lange," he said.

And then it happened. A sneeze. Ethan groaned. *Why is it always a sneeze that gives you away to the bad guys?* That little sneeze was enough to alert the three gunmen. *Letting Vakh think that Sarah was my family was a mistake.* Sarah had become Vakh's enemy merely by her association with Ethan.

Grasping a fistful of Ethan's hair, Foghorn dragged him across the hall to the Special Collections room while Miguel and another man trained their rifles at Ethan's head. Shoving Ethan to his knees and instructing him to lace his fingers behind his head, Foghorn investigated the sneeze.

Soon, discovered and threatened by Foghorn, Sarah emerged, her boys held tightly in her arms, a look of fierceness in her eyes. She walked as instructed surely understanding that resistance would only endanger the children.

Vakh made a noise deep in his chest as he circled Sarah and the little boys. Ethan clamped his teeth together to prevent acting on the instinct to protect.

"You surprise me once again, Mr. Lange," Vakh said. He snapped his fingers and two of his men forced Ethan and the little family toward and then up the stairs.

Topping the first flight of stairs, Ethan approached the fire doors ahead of Sarah and the boys and inspiration blazed a trail across his mind. *Exit.* With only a vague plan in his mind, Ethan acted, thrusting his body to the right, slamming into Miguel, hearing the man's grunt as his head smacked against the corner. Pushing off his body, Ethan reached forward to rip the gun from another man in front of him firing twice behind him to send Foghorn diving for cover.

Spinning, Ethan grabbed Sarah and the boys, flinging them against the fire door, effectively ejecting them from the building. The alarmed doors buzzed in protest of the unauthorized exit. Ethan saw Sarah trip and then catch her balance, glancing back briefly before following his instructions.

"RUN!" Ethan shouted just before he was flung forward onto his knees. A rifle smacked him in the face, snapping his head around to see many more than three joining the struggle. Fighting back, still woozy from the blow to his head, Ethan tried to block the kicks and punches to his ribs, his head and shoulders as he gradually lost consciousness.

CHAPTER 2

Sarah ran. The corner was just there and then she'd be out of range. The sharp report of a rifle sounded and her heart accelerated to a gallop when she felt warmth spread along her side. *It would hurt if I'd been shot, wouldn't it?* Pulling Charlie and Teddy closer, she prayed that the hot liquid on her side did not indicate that the bullet had found a target in either her body or her sons'.

Leaning into the corner, her breath harsh in her ears, she forced herself onward. There at the edge of the building stood people, stood freedom. Suddenly, between there and here, a huge man covered in black loomed before her, his gun at his side, his face hidden behind a black helmet and mask. Startled at first, Sarah quickly realized that this anonymous man was police not terrorist.

The SWAT officer grasped her upper arm and drew her toward the crowd. When she felt the prickle of pursuit lessen, Sarah pulled out of the officer's grip and dropped to her knees. Setting her sons to stand in front of her, she rapidly surveyed their little bodies for bullet holes. She found only that Charlie had wet himself. Sighing deeply in relief, she hugged them to her.

Standing again, Sarah turned her attention to the officer. "I need…to speak with …someone in charge," she said.

"Come with me, ma'am. You're safe now," her black-helmeted rescuer assured her, gesturing for her to precede him to the paramedics stationed near three ambulances.

She dug in her heels, pulling free of his hold. "You don't understand. I was with Ethan Lange, clearance code 99672…"

"I don't know what that means, ma'am. Please follow me," he insisted, his voice losing the conciliatory tone it had held previously.

"Listen!" Sarah insisted. "I don't know what it means either but he's someone important. Ethan Lange."

Sarah caught sight of a young woman striding toward her. *Who's that and what does she want with me?* Tall and slender, the woman carried a command in her tone and confidence in her stature; fair of face but stern of nature. Tossing her raven hair over her shoulder, the woman intruded into the interchange.

"Excuse me. Who did you say you were with?" she asked Sarah.

"Ethan Lange. Clearance code—" Sarah began but the woman cut her off with a gesture.

"Never mind that, come with me. I'll take over, officer." The woman turned to speak to the SWAT officer who backed off at the flash of her identification, muttering about "nightcrawlers".

The dark haired woman was speaking to her again. "My name is Isabella Farini. I'm a colleague of Ethan's. Come with me and tell me what happened."

"Gladly, but I need to change Charlie. He's had an accident. He's soaking wet," Sarah said.

"It looks as though you're a little damp as well," Isabella said as her gaze traveled over Sarah and the boys.

"Yes." Sarah released a dry chuckle. "But I'll keep. He's shivering." *Probably as much in shock as cold. My poor boys.*

As Sarah followed Isabella to a black Ford Explorer, she surveyed the shocked expressions on her children's faces. Isabella opened a rear door and Sarah set Charlie behind it to give him a little privacy. She pulled a change of clothes out of her pack as well as a bag of wipes and began to strip, clean and dress Charlie. Teddy sat on the floor of the vehicle beside her as she worked, remaining quiet as Sarah told Isabella everything she'd heard and experienced.

Bella interrupted with questions, urgency in her voice and manner. "You say that the one gunman stood out from the others. What do you mean?" Isabella asked.

"Well, the other gunmen were regular thugs, unkempt, scruffy. He was obviously carefully groomed. I think there was even product in his hair. His clothes matched the style of the others but were clearly made of a finer material," Sarah said.

Sarah pulled the newly dressed Charlie into her arms for a hug. After that, she tucked him into the seat behind her. Almost immediately, she felt his warmth against her back as he draped his arms over her shoulders, pressing his cheek to her neck. Teddy reached for her, resting his hand on her knee as he sat, cross-legged on the floor beside her.

Sarah continued, "The other men were definitely Americans, from the southern States I would guess, but he, the leader, definitely didn't sound American or Canadian."

"If you saw a picture, would you recognize him?" Isabella asked.

Sarah nodded. *Oh, yes. I will definitely remember that man for a very long time.*

Bella pulled out her cell phone and connected. "Owen, it's Bella. I need you. Very funny." She slid it shut, ending the call abruptly. "Did Ethan seem to know any of the men?"

"I think so. It was hard to tell because I couldn't hear everything but it seemed like the leader, the tidy man, recognized Ethan. He called him by name," Sarah said.

Sarah noticed that Bella didn't really seem to be a part of all the police activity around them but rather sat as an island within it. "What is going on?" Sarah asked. "Will Ethan be okay? He saved our lives. Bella, he doesn't know us from Adam or Eve but he put himself in the line of danger to protect us."

"Ethan Lange takes his job very seriously," Bella said as she gave Sarah's shoulder a gentle squeeze.

Soon a young man arrived, tall, slender, buzzed hair, handing a PDA to Bella. She passed it over to Sarah. "Is this the man who saved you?" Bella asked.

The man in the picture had short blonde hair as pale as Charlie's and a rugged, tanned face with high cheekbones, a grim mouth and a narrow nose which had been broken at least once. He was a handsome man with the bluest eyes. Sarah nodded. "Yes, that's Ethan. He seemed so very sad and then he asked me an odd question…and then he saved us."

Bella switched the picture on the screen and showed Sarah another man. "Have a look at this. Is this the man who held you captive? Our refined terrorist?" Bella asked.

Sarah recognized him instantly. "Yes. That's him."

The young man, Owen, responded, "That's not good, Farini. Borz Vakh, Chechen mercenary. Isn't he the one who Ethan—"

"Yeah. I told you we needed to be here," Bella cut him off. "The—"

Her next words were interrupted by gunfire in the building followed by a mass reaction of the SWAT team. Flinching at the reminder of the proximity of danger, Sarah instinctively clutched Teddy and Charlie to her.

"Stay here!" Bella ordered and then she and Owen were gone.

"Mommy?" Teddy asked. "Will they go get Ethan?"

"They'll try, sweetheart," Sarah replied, smiling grimly at her tender-hearted son.

"He scared me," Teddy said.

"I think maybe Ethan only scared us to save us," she said.

The cyclone of confusion swirled around them and Sarah moved into the back seat of the car, pulling the door closed and giving the boys a snack of raisins and apple juice before laying them down on the seats and singing them to sleep. As the terrorists exited in handcuffs, in raced the paramedics and soon Sarah saw three people wheeled out on stretchers. Ethan was one of the three.

First checking on her children, assuring herself that they were still sleeping soundly, Sarah then made her way to Ethan's side. He was pale and beaten, bruises and welts visible across his tanned and chiseled features, his strong and battered body covered by a sheet. *Poor man.* Surprising herself, she brushed her fingers through his close-cropped blonde hair seeking to comfort the one who had saved her children, the one given away to punishment because of a tiny boy sneeze. She had no idea what kind of man he was except that he was courageous and he deserved her gratitude.

Ethan's eyes fluttered open, widening slightly, she thought, when he saw her. It was hard to tell with all the swelling around his eyes.

"Are the little boys safe?" Ethan asked. His voice was breathy and low.

"Yes. Thank you. Thank you for saving us. You were very brave," Sarah said.

He nodded once, his strong chin bobbing. "No problem," Ethan said; a comment which Sarah found oddly out of step with his injuries. "What are their names?"

"Teddy and Charlie," she said.

Ethan nodded again and then he closed his eyes. Resting her hand on his shoulder, she tried to transmit comfort to him as he awaited the paramedics.

"Sarah!" Sarah turned at her name to see Bella waving her back to the car.

Sarah murmured, "Thank you, Ethan," giving his shoulder one last pat before moving back to the Ford Explorer that contained her sleeping children. "Does he have someone to stay with him at the hospital?" Sarah asked, gesturing behind her.

"Who? Ethan?" Bella exchanged a look with Owen. "No. No one."

"I'd like to then. A little kindness seems a fair exchange for such courage. He would be unharmed if it weren't for us," Sarah said.

Owen replied to that. "Unlikely. He spends his life associated with violence."

"Very poetic, Owen, but not really relevant," Bella said. "We're stopping off at the hospital on our way to the office. You can ride with us."

Ethan and the other two victims of the terrorists were taken into the Emergency Room and treated immediately. Sarah waited until Bella came to fetch her, telling her that Ethan had a concussion, three cracked ribs and stitches over his right eye and beneath his chin. He was bruised, essentially, from his shoulders to his toes.

Sarah, Teddy and Charlie took up a post in Ethan's room. *I'm not really sure what I hope to accomplish here but the thought of him waking alone in the hospital just seems so...sad.* Tucking the boys into the overstuffed chair in the corner of the hospital room, Sarah wrapped them in a powder blue blanket. Then she took a hard-backed chair and positioned it between the boys and the man.

Ethan's mind emerged toward consciousness before his limbs felt able to move. *What happened?* He remembered stepping into the Sculpture room of the National Gallery, morbidly drawn to Rodin's *The Kiss* depicting the passionate embrace of deep love. *At what point in my life did I decide that I didn't need love?*

"Mommy, look! They're kissing!" A small boy had run up to the sculpture, planting his little hand on the sculpted man's foot.

"Yes," his mother had replied, smiling down at the little boy.

That had been Ethan's first glimpse of Sarah, looking over to see a thirty-something woman, her almond-shaped eyes set in a heart-shaped face that lifted easily into a smile when she gazed at her children. Ethan had watched her readjust the pack on her back, the pack overflowing with stuffed animals, toys dinosaurs, juice boxes and granola bars. He felt an unfamiliar warmth in his chest at the memory of the loving mother answering the questions of her older son as her younger son sat on her hip playing with the long ends of her chestnut brown hair. Her bright red sweater and denim skirt made her appear ready for action and gently sweet at the same time.

"Are they in love?" the older boy had asked.

"I expect so," she'd replied.

"What's the biggest love, Mommy?" he'd asked.

"Greater love has no one than he who lays down his life for a friend," she'd said.

Greater love... Those words brought the memory of other words to Ethan's mind. *'You don't have the first idea about love. I could never be with you. No one could, because you would never give up a piece of your heart.'* Brigitte's words, when she'd walked out on him ten years ago.

Ethan hadn't intended to walk away from love but the choices he'd made in his personal and professional life seemed to have disqualified him from romance and passion. An undercover officer who spent his days infiltrating terrorist organizations had no right to a personal life anyway, did he?

Unable to escape the mother's words, Ethan had stepped toward the little family. "Who said that?" he'd asked.

Cautiously, the mother had replied and for the first time he'd noticed the warmth of her deep brown, velvety eyes. "Jesus, actually. He definitely was the authority on true love."

Ethan had snorted, drawing a frown from the mother. "True love," he'd sneered. "What is that, really?"

"Putting another's needs ahead of your own; giving up a piece of yourself to make them happy; choosing to love even in the unlovely moments. Wouldn't you agree that Jesus pretty much sums that up?" she'd said as though challenging him to prove her wrong.

Ethan had nodded, stepping away, listening to the little boy chattering again. Chattering. Noise. Beeping. The beeping drew Ethan from his memories. *Hospital? Not again!* Ethan hated hospitals. They represented inactivity and too much time to think.

Inhaling tentatively, Ethan was confused by the scent of baby powder and lavender which invaded his senses. Turning toward the bouquet of gentleness, his body protested as a piercing pain flashed across his chest and shoulders.

"Ruddy terrorists," he muttered.

"Pardon me?"

Ethan's eyes flew open at the sound of a woman's voice. *Brigitte? Bella? No...*"Sarah, is it?" he asked.

"Yes. Hello, Ethan," she said.

"What happened? Where are the little boys, Teddy and...?" he asked.

"Charlie," Sarah said. "You saved us. And I guess they beat you for it. I don't really know what happened after you tossed us out the fire door."

"Why are you here?" he asked, probably more forcefully than necessary. He couldn't understand her presence in his hospital room or the warmth that permeated his chest at the sight of her.

She seemed taken aback by his question. "They said you had no one to sit with you. After what you did, I couldn't let you wake alone in a hospital bed." Her voice began to freeze over. "I'll leave now since you clearly don't—"

Reaching out, he clutched her sleeve. "Thank you. I don't mean to be...ungrateful."

She released a dry chuckle. "You certainly don't have anything to be grateful for. But we do, and I wanted to thank you. So thank you. We'll leave—"

They were interrupted by Owen Cullen's arrival. "Hey, boss! Couldn't keep out of trouble, huh?" the young man offered with a grin. Ethan sighed. *Once the enquiry is over, will I ever see my team again?*

The younger boy, Charlie, was awakened by Owen's boisterous joking. Crawling down from the chair, the sleepy boy ran to his mother, clinging to her skirt. She turned and picked him up, reassuring him quietly.

"What's happening?" Ethan demanded to know, ignoring Owen's teasing.

Owen sobered. "They've collected the witnesses and transported them to the Washington Plaza until they can all be questioned. Once that's completed, we'll know whether or not we got all of the terrorists."

Ethan noticed Sarah collecting her things, putting Charlie down in order to rouse the older boy. "Come on, Teddy, we need to go now," she murmured sweetly.

Charlie trotted over to the hospital bed, climbing the rails like a jungle gym, coming to rest, kneeling beside Ethan. He planted his hand in the middle of Ethan's battered chest and leaned into his face.

"Bye-bye Ethan," he said, except he pronounced it "Eefan", and then leaned forward and kissed Ethan on the chin. Charlie dropped back to the floor and ran over to take his mother's free hand. Her face wore a mixed expression of astonishment and amusement as Ethan reached up to wipe the apple juice from his chin, an equal mixture of emotions in his mind.

Ethan watched them as they exited, feeling a brief sense of loss when they passed out of the room, Teddy looking back once to wave. *Why do I even care if I never see them again? I did my job by saving them.* Attempting to close his emotions back into their requisite compartments, Ethan felt them slip free when the door opened again. *I hardly know them. Why am I pleased that they would return?* But the lightness was replaced by apprehension as Bella rather than Sarah hurried into the room.

"What's happened?" Ethan asked, his heart accelerating to match his sense of foreboding.

"They've been murdered. All of the witnesses have been murdered," Bella replied, her voice tight, her hands fisted.

Ethan braced his arm across his ribs, struggling to sit upright, making it only a fraction of the angle. "What do you mean?" he said.

"Someone, two men, got into the suite where the witnesses were waiting to give their statements to the police. The gunmen opened fire," Bella said, clearly shaken up. Her voice was shaking. "Two officers were injured and all of the witnesses were killed. The Director has ordered us to take you into protective custody."

"Me. Why me?" Ethan asked, confused.

Bella smiled grimly. "You're the sole remaining witness. They'll need your testimony."

"And?" Ethan asked, suspicious of the message left unsaid.

"And a gunman was spotted twenty minutes ago trying to enter the hospital through the Morgue. A security guard frightened him off," Bella said.

Ethan blanched. *I'm not the only witness.* "Sarah." Ethan leveraged himself higher in the bed. "Go and get her. Bella, get her and bring her back." Bella studied him for a moment so he clarified. "I'm not the only witness."

Bella's eyes widened and she spun on her heel, accelerating down the hall.

CHAPTER 3

Sarah was exhausted. The turmoil of the day weighed heavily on her now that she was almost free of it. *Ethan is a cold but brave man. Well, I did what I came to do: be there when he woke and thank him for saving our lives. Now, back to the hotel, I guess, for a shower and sleep. I hope Charlie can sleep now after those naps.*

"Mama. Sing *Arky-Arky.* Pease?" Charlie asked, his upturned eyes pleading.

Sarah chuckled. *No rest for the weary.* She began to sing quietly, aware of the hospital patients sleeping in the rooms around them. The boys joined in. Trying to keep them singing, Sarah was increasingly concerned about a man in surgical scrubs who was bearing down on them. His gaze intent, he held his right arm behind him as though carrying something against the small of his back.

Teddy interrupted her, his voice grave as though delivering the tidings of apocalypse. "Mommy, I needa go pee."

Beginning to search around for the ladies' symbol, she assured him they'd find a washroom.

"Sarah!"

Sarah turned to see Bella jogging toward her, motioning urgently for her to wait. The man in scrubs had disappeared.

"Mommy! I needa pee," Teddy insisted.

"Just a minute, son," Sarah replied, turning back to Bella. "Look, Bella? Teddy needs to go to the washroom. And really, I've been soaked once already."

"You don't understand, Sarah, I need you to return to Ethan's room with me now," Bella said tersely.

"Mom~my!" Teddy said, turning the word into five syllables. Pulling on Sarah's arm, he danced around.

"Teddy, stop," Sarah said. "Bella, I need to find a washroom. Now! Help me or clean up the puddle. Your choice!"

"Here." Bella led them around the corner to the right and then—oh, glory be!—to a toilet. Bella insisted on checking the space and then finally let the little boy relieve himself. Sarah shook her head in amusement at the loud sigh Teddy emitted as he emptied his bladder.

Once the boys had each taken a turn with the toilet and their little hands were washed clean of gummy bears and apple juice, Sarah led them out into the hallway to greet a nervously pacing Bella.

"Okay, Sarah, I need you to come with me now," Bella said.

"Look, Bella," Sarah said in mounting frustration. "I'm tired. The boys are cranky. I'm covered in urine and apple juice and all I really want is a shower and a change of clothes. I'm not interested in who your boss is or what he's involved in. I just want to go to my hotel room and sleep."

"Sleep Mommy?" Teddy said.

"Hotel Mama!" Charlie said.

Bella tried again. "Come back with me and I can explain." Then she lowered her voice as though children couldn't hear whispers. "I don't want to frighten them," Bella said, pointing at Teddy and Charlie.

Sarah studied her, taking so long to decide that Charlie started to swing from her arm and Teddy started to try and pull the pack off her back so he could locate...something. She groaned.

"Teddy, what do you want? Charlie, stop and stand up properly."

As Teddy began to answer, Sarah's chest clenched. There he was again, the man in scrubs and he was definitely moving directly towards them, menace in his every step.

"Bella, look!" Sarah nodded her head in the direction of the man as she began to back away.

"Sarah, run!" Bella shouted.

Sarah spun, dragging the two boys with her, left and then right and then left again until Sarah didn't have any idea where they were headed. The boys ran along at her side. An elevator opened to the left of them and she darted in, hurriedly tapping the down button. Ducking down as the man came around the corner, Sarah screamed as a bullet pinged into the wall just over her head. Her heart accelerated. If she hadn't ducked, she would have been shot.

What should she do? She wasn't an agent. She didn't know what to do when men shot at you! How did this happen? She just wanted to take the boys on the vacation that she and David had planned to take. Why did she ever have to meet Ethan Lange?

The ping of the elevator as it reached the main floor reminded Sarah that now was the time for action not recrimination. Tucking the boys behind her against the front wall of the elevator, she reached out, trapping the door open, scanning the foyer for help…and the man with the gun. There by the double sliding doors of the main entrance stood a security guard. Carefully keeping watch for danger, she crept out of the elevator toward the guard, the boys' hands firmly in hers.

"Sarah, get down!"

Pulling the boys into the nurse's station, Sarah covered them with her body. *I'm sure that was Ethan's voice.*

"Freeze!" Ethan's voice again and Sarah peeked out to see him clad in a hospital gown, jeans and bare feet, a gun in his hand. He swayed where he stood and she wondered how he remained upright.

"Sir, lower your weapon." That must have been the security guard.

"FBI. This man is under arrest. Do you have handcuffs, er, Filbert?" Ethan said.

"Sir, I need to see some identification," said Filbert? Was the man's name really Filbert?

"Owen. Show him some ID," Ethan said tersely.

The security guard came into view but as he moved toward Owen, he crossed the path between Ethan and the gunman. A shot fired and Sarah saw Ethan fall hard. Two more shots and the screaming morass of patients undulated around Sarah, Teddy and Charlie.

"Sarah!" Bella's voice came through the noise. "Sarah, are you all right?"

Sarah peeked around the corner of the nurse's station, finally emerging at Bella's reassurance. "*Now* will you accompany me to Ethan's room?" Bella asked.

Sarah blinked in disbelief, looking down into the widened eyes of her sons and nodding.

"Ethan?" Sarah asked, her voice quivering with fear and uncertainty.

Bella nodded in his direction and Sarah watched as Ethan argued with the orderly trying to put him in a wheelchair to return him to his room. There was no blood on him. So he'd not been shot. Turning, she saw the terrorist surrounded by medical personnel, and the security guard, Filbert, above him, handcuffs in hand.

Redirecting her focus, Bella turned Sarah away and shrugged in Ethan's direction. "We'll meet him upstairs," Bella said. "If they can get him to sit down."

As they reached the elevator, Charlie began to whimper, pulling back on Sarah's arm.

"No, mama. No," Charlie said.

"It's okay, Charlie. The elevator's safe now," Sarah said, hugging him against her leg.

Shaking his head, Charlie continued to pull back.

"Charlie," Bella said, crouching down in front of him. "Is that your name?"

Charlie stopped pulling, forcing his body flush against his mother's leg.

"Do you know that I have a cat named Charlie?" Bella said.

"Kitty cat?" Charlie said. Sarah watched Bella carefully.

"Yes. Would you like to see a picture of him?" Bella asked, reaching into her pocket to retrieve her PDA. Charlie nodded vigorously in affirmation. She pressed a few buttons and then presented the photo to Charlie. Teddy peeked out from the other side of Sarah and looked over Bella's shoulder at the pretty calico.

"He's fat," Teddy said.

Bella chuckled, agreeing as she walked slowly back into the elevator, holding her PDA down where the boys could see it. Up two floors, they debarked and Bella coaxed them toward Ethan's room. Teddy jogged ahead and then stopped to check in with his mother. Once Teddy received the nod, Charlie ran ahead with him to see the next picture that Bella presented. Sarah shook her head in amusement colored by exasperation…and followed.

Arriving at Ethan's room, Sarah was surprised to see him in the bed but not surprised by the deep scowl on his features.

"Hi, Eefan." Charlie greeted him cheerily, skipping over to climb up onto the hospital bed again, sitting cross-legged beside Ethan. Teddy slowed at the door, fisting Sarah's skirt and waving cautiously from her side.

"Now, may I ask what is going on? Why my children and I are chased through hospitals? Why we are not allowed to return to our hotel room?" Sarah asked, her frustration slipping into her voice despite her best efforts.

"Sarah, we need you to—"

Owen began to explain but Sarah cut him off, enunciating each word clearly so there could be no mistake of her feelings. "Owen? I have had enough of this day," she said. "I'm weary and worn and I want a shower, clothes that don't stink of pee and a hot bath. Wait, I only need a shower or a bath, not both. What I mean to say is—"

"Sarah," Ethan said, raising a hand as though to stop her tirade.

She pointed at him. "DON'T interrupt me!"

Ethan subsided into shocked silence and Charlie turned to pat him sympathetically on the cheek. "You in twubba now," he informed Ethan who released the tension on a single laugh.

"What is going on?" Sarah demanded to know.

Ethan took a breath, interrupted by a wince at the pull on his battered ribs. "The other witnesses are D-E-A-D," he replied simply, spelling out the word. He glanced meaningfully at the two children.

Shock stilled Sarah's body and mind. *Dead?* Eventually, she cleared her throat to force her vocal chords into action. "But the man downstairs? If he's—are we still in D-A-N-G-E-R?"

Bella intruded, speaking to Ethan. "No one seems to know they even exist. They're not listed as hostages or as witnesses."

"We have to protect them, because the terrorists obviously know they're here," Ethan insisted quietly, his expression intractable.

"We would need to sneak them into the same safe house as you in order to keep it secret. If we place them somewhere else, we'd have to explain it and file a report," Bella said.

Ethan nodded slowly. "Arrange it. And get me out of here."

"You're not really fit to be released, Ethan," Sarah intruded seriously.

Bella turned to Sarah as she explained, "There's no choice. We can't protect him here."

"It's not up to either of you when I choose to check myself out of hospital," Ethan asserted hotly.

Sarah turned a narrowed gaze on him. "Exactly who do you think you are? The Maharajah of Mysore? If the doctor says you need care, then you need care."

"You have no right—" Ethan spluttered in reply.

"Sarah," Bella interrupted. "We can't protect him here and we can't take the risk of involving another person in his care."

"Fine. Then you get the materials and instructions from the doctor and I'll look after him," Sarah stated, not particularly happy with the idea.

"You don't owe me anything," Ethan replied hotly.

Sarah's temper fired. "You shut up and—"

"Mommy, you said the 's' word!" Teddy admonished her.

"Oh, for goodness' sake," she mumbled, blushing red.

But Ethan laughed as heartily, it seemed, as his battered ribs would allow. "That's a slam dunk, Teddy," Ethan said. "Bella, make the arrangements. Owen, go to the hotel and get their things. Now, find me a doctor and get me out of here."

CHAPTER 4

Once the arrangements were made, Sarah, the boys and Ethan were delivered to the top floor apartment of a Brownstone walk-up set in the middle of a block of apartments. The neighboring flats vibrated with a weirdly synchronous mix of Rap and Metal. Upon arriving, Sarah watched Ethan silently shuffle, pale and bent, past the kitchen on the right and the washroom on the left and into the second bedroom.

Wearily hauling the drowsy boys into the first bedroom, Sarah released them onto the creaking mattress and then removed their trousers, socks and shoes. In relief, she rolled them under the covers and then slid in beside them, falling asleep almost immediately.

The next morning, Sarah rose at the break of dawn because Teddy and Charlie thought the early morning was positively the best time to be awake. She didn't see Ethan again until midmorning when he emerged dressed in well-worn jeans and a plain blue t-shirt which stretched across his chest. He looked slightly less pale but much more abused as the bruises had deepened from red to purple in the night. The bandages covering the stitches over his eyebrow and beneath his chin stood out against the pallor of his face.

Scowling broodily, Ethan shuffled past Teddy and Charlie who were playing *tigers* on the carpet and then made his way first to the washroom and then the kitchen to make a pot of coffee. Trying desperately, ridiculously, to ignore her and the boys, Ethan moved about, pouring the coffee, trying to carry the newspaper, a plate of toast and a mug into the lounge and failing miserably. Growling, he abandoned the toast and paper and carried the mug in one hand, his other arm clutched across his aching ribs.

Stubborn man. Sarah watched him settle on the sofa, shoving aside the toys and books on the coffee table and propping his bare feet there. Once he settled, she carried over the newspaper, the toast and some sliced melon, setting them beside him without a word. Immediately, Teddy stood up from where he was seated on the floor in front of the television and handed Ethan the remote control.

"Mommy, will you play *Go Fish?*" Teddy asked her before he darted into the bedroom to retrieve his playing cards.

Charlie followed his big brother and then emerged with an armload of books, dumping them on the sofa and curling up to "read" to Ethan. Watching his brow furrow, Sarah wondered what he was thinking. How was he going to deal with the fact that small children don't simply disappear? She shook off the thoughts wearily. She had quite enough to deal with without having to concern herself with the man.

Preparing supper later, Sarah stood over the pot of chili watching Ethan try to ignore the three of them, using his scowl as a barrier of protection. Turning off the stove, Sarah pulled the biscuits she'd made out of the oven and placed them on the table with the chili.

"Supper's ready!" she said, her announcement met by cheers from the boys and no response from Ethan. "Ethan, supper's ready."

Glancing over, he replied tonelessly, "You don't need to cook for me."

"Irritating man," she mumbled, fed up with his attitude. Serving the boys first, she then filled a bowl with chili, adding two buttered biscuits. Taking it over to Ethan, she placed it on the coffee table without a word.

"You don't need to cook for me," he said again, his eyes fixed on the television.

"Is this how it's going to work?" she asked, hands on her hips.

"What do you mean?" he asked, suspiciously meeting her gaze.

"You pretend we don't exist and we try to live as though you're not insufferably rude?" she asked, daring him to answer.

Ethan's expression blanked. "It's not that I don't appreciate your kindness, it's just that it's not necessary. You don't owe me anything."

"Well, in fact I do owe you quite a lot but that's not why I cooked supper for you. We're together in this rundown apartment for who knows how long. Why shouldn't we cooperate? Didn't you learn anything from watching Sesame Street?" she said.

Ethan laughed once in astonishment, "I guess I forgot," and then continued, his voice lower, "I don't want you to do this because you feel obligated."

Sarah wondered what that comment revealed about the deep thoughts of Ethan Lange. "I don't feel obligated, Ethan," she said, her voice softer now. "Just grateful. Please, just eat the chili and tell me if you like it. Maybe soon you'll be well enough to join us at the table. The boys would like that."

Ethan sighed and seemed to think about her words for a moment. "All right." He shifted upright on the sofa, reaching for the bowl. The movement brought him up short with a gasp of pain.

"I don't mind if you ask me for help, you know," she said, picking up the bowl and taking it to the supper table.

Ethan shuffled over and joined them.

"Who wants to ask the blessing?" Sarah asked and Ethan looked up in surprise, returning the spoonful he'd just lifted to his mouth to the bowl.

"Me. Me," Teddy volunteered. Sarah, Teddy and Charlie bowed their heads. "God is great. God is good. And we thank him for this food. Amen."

"Thank you, son," she said. "Dig in."

Ethan remained motionless until Teddy and Charlie began to partake. Sarah chatted with the boys about what they'd seen in Washington since arriving ten days ago. Ethan remained silent, accepting seconds when Sarah offered them and thanking her politely. After supper, he helped clear up, one dish at a time along with the boys.

Once the sink was filled with hot, soapy water and the dishes inserted, Sarah dried her arms and asked Teddy to fetch some playing cards so they could teach Charlie how to play memory. Ethan stood back watching them, his gaze flat and unreadable.

"Eefan?" Tugging on Ethan's trouser leg, Charlie looked up to the heights of the man's lanky six foot frame. "Wanna pay?"

To Sarah's surprise, she detected a flash of something in the man's eyes.

"Uh, no," Ethan said, his voice gruff.

Charlie's gaze fell to the floor in disappointment and Sarah's heart clenched in sorrow for her son. *Why can't he open up just a little? Charlie is trying so hard.*

"Come on, Charlie. Ethan's not feeling well. Maybe he'll play another time," Sarah said, turning her back on the man, dismissing him.

"Okay," Charlie conceded sadly.

They played *Memory* for half an hour and then Sarah found a few plastic bowls in the cupboard to create a volcanic landscape on the table for Teddy's dinosaurs and the three of them played for another hour until she finally conceded to the need to finish the dishes, bathe the boys and put them to bed. She decided to stay in the bedroom and read rather than go out and sit beside Ethan, pretending he didn't exist.

Over the next two days, Ethan surreptitiously observed the little family. Sarah cooked and looked after the children and Ethan tried not to succumb to the melancholy encroaching on his heart. It had been so long since he'd witnessed *normal* life that he felt like he was watching a foreign film where words and actions carried a meaning to which he had no insight or frame of reference. The loving interaction between Sarah and her sons pulled at his heart, reminding him of another mother who had loved her sons.

The younger one, Charlie, kept inviting him to read or listen or play and Ethan found that it did take his mind off the pain in his ribs and the anxiety over the upcoming enquiry. So he began to occasionally say 'yes' when Charlie asked him. *Only because it makes the kid easier to deal with*, he told himself. He even let Teddy watch cartoons, noticing that the boy never came too close to him, probably still a little afraid after being grabbed in the gallery.

"Ethan." Sarah's voice coming from the apartment door interrupted his thoughts. "Isn't the password supposed to change every day?" she asked.

"Yes," he replied, looking up from the book he was reading to Charlie, pausing at *C* is for *caribou*.

"There's someone here giving yesterday's password. Should I let him in?" she asked.

"Do you recognize the agent?" Ethan said as he set Charlie aside, stepped over Teddy's dinosaurs and approached the door. He braced his ribs with his arm until his muscles eased enough so he could straighten fully.

"No." Sarah paused, stepping up on tiptoes to see better from her five foot, four inch height. "There are two of them but I can only see the one fellow's face. He's got something in his hand."

"Get away from the door, Sarah! Get back!" Ethan said, the bells of warning clanging.

"Why? Just tell me—"

In two more steps, he reached the door, grasping Sarah's arm and pulling her away from the entrance.

"Just get back," he said, raising his voice to try and hurry her compliance. Looking through the peephole, Ethan recognized danger long before he saw the stun grenade in the man's hand. "Get my gun, Sarah. It's on the nightstand."

Trusting her to follow through, Ethan tipped the kitchen table and pushed it against the door with his shoulder. He swallowed a groan at the pull it out on his ribs. The table was solid oak. Heavy. It would hopefully create a barrier to keep the bad guys away from Sarah and the little boys.

"What's going on?" Sarah asked as she pressed Ethan's Glock into his hand.

"Get the boys. Go into the bedroom and hide under the bed," Ethan said. His voice was calm and authoritative as he settled back into the professional groove. "Now! Before it's too late."

Without pause, Sarah spun away to gather the boys into the safety of the bedroom. He hoped.

Ethan leaned up to see through the peephole. *Yikes!* He lurched aside just in time as an axe rent the apartment door. Following the axe, a stun grenade arced through the new opening and Ethan dove for the bathroom, landing on his side. His ribs exploded in agony. Fighting the waves of blackness that assaulted him, he kicked the door shut and covered his face with a bath towel just before the flash-bang detonated. Only a small portion of the intense flash filtered under the door and the concussive noise was greatly dimmed by the barrier of wood and terry cloth.

Fighting down the nausea from the pain assaulting his chest, Ethan cracked the bathroom door open, catching glimpses of a black-clad figure wielding an axe at the quickly diminishing door. Lying on his back, aiming between his knees, Ethan set up a shot and fired six shots in rapid succession just as sirens sounded in the distance. One or the other sent the axe-man and his comrade fleeing.

Pushing back the gray at the edges of his vision and struggling to his feet, Ethan moved to the door cautiously but the axe-man was well and truly gone. Wetting a kitchen towel under the faucet, he dropped it on the smoldering edges of the plastic table cloth, nearly ignited by the flash-bang of the stun grenade.

With nothing more to do until the police walked through the savaged door, Ethan walked to the first bedroom, rapping on the door.

"Sarah, it's safe. Are you okay?" Ethan said.

Opening the door slowly, Sarah emerged, her face revealing the myriad of emotions she'd experienced.

"What happened?" she asked, her voice quivering. "Smoke? Is there a fire? Were there gunshots?"

Ignoring the specifics of her questions, he sought to reassure her. "They're gone. The sirens frightened them away." Thoughtfully, Ethan paused. "I wonder who called the cops."

"I did," she said, holding out her cell phone to him, the operator still on the line, her tinny voice calling through the tiny speaker. Ethan took the phone, ending the call.

"Are *you* okay? Are you hurt?" she asked, brushing splinters from his shirt.

Ethan shook his head, startled by her question. *How long has it been since anyone's cared what happened to me?*

"Where are the boys?" Ethan asked. "Are they okay?"

"Teddy, Charlie, come out. It's safe now. Ethan scared away the bad men," Sarah said.

The little boys crept out from under the bed and then launched themselves at their mother's legs. She lifted them into her arms and Ethan felt an unfamiliar sensation in his belly, a longing for something he hadn't had since his mother had died when he was seven. The middle of three brothers, he'd been left behind with his cold and distant father.

A soft pat on his shoulder drew his attention from his thoughts.

"Hug, Eefan?" Charlie asked and dropped himself into Ethan's arms so that Ethan was forced to take him or let him fall to the floor. Bracing Charlie on his hip to avoid the pull on his ribs, Ethan accepted the boy's tight hug and loud kiss.

"Thank you, Ethan. You've saved us again," Sarah said gratefully, kissing him lightly on the cheek.

"Thank you, Ethan," Teddy mimicked his mother, reaching over to hug Ethan but remaining in Sarah's arms.

Tamping down the unfamiliar emotions, Ethan blanked his expression. Soon the apartment was filled with police officers and his former officers, the incorrigible Owen Cullen and the hard-edged Isabella Farini.

"Lange, man, you all right?" Owen asked, clapping him on the shoulder. Ethan flinched at the jolt of pain the movement ignited in his injured ribs. Bella just looked shocked for some reason Ethan couldn't identify until he realized how out of character it was for him to be seen in public offering comfort, to a child nonetheless. He was known to his colleagues as a ruthless agent, self-assured and independent.

"What happened here, sir?" a police officer named Knight asked. "We got a 911 call about an intruder."

"Yes," Ethan said, indicating the door as he continued, "As you can see, our intruder is long gone." Asking Sarah to take the boys into the kitchen while he spoke to the officers, Ethan filled the police in on the details of the break-in and then pulled Owen and Bella aside for a conference.

"Was it the Chechen?" Bella asked.

"No way to know. There were two individuals. Sarah saw the one...you'll need to get a description. The other was dressed in black. His face was covered with a balaclava. It was a male, most likely, about five-ten, five-eleven, obviously strong enough to break through the door with an axe. And someone with enough access to intelligence to find us here," Ethan said, adding in a mutter, "Flash-bangs aren't exactly easy to come by either, but on the other hand, not difficult to obtain if you know where to shop."

"Did you get him?" Owen asked, making a bang-bang gesture with his hand.

Shrugging one shoulder, Ethan said, "I fired six shots. If there's a bullet unaccounted for, there's a good chance it's lodged in one of them."

Nodding toward the kitchen, Ethan instructed Bella to bring Sarah over to provide a description of the man impersonating a security officer.

Sarah returned with Bella, carrying a glass for Ethan. "I brought you some lemonade. And…and a cookie." He watched her in astonishment, taking the lemonade and draining it in one gulp, handing the glass back to her and taking the cookie. Her eyes pleaded with him for reassurance or comfort or something that he didn't have it in him to give.

"Sarah—" he began but she cut him off, brushing away his words and said, "I'm fine. There's no need."

Ethan glanced over toward the kitchen where the boys were being entertained by the burly Constable Knight. Teddy was wearing the officer's hat and Charlie was riding his baton around the kitchen like a hobby horse.

When Ethan turned back to his former colleagues, Bella was watching him with a curious expression on her face.

"What?" he asked gruffly.

"Nothing," she replied, blanking her face of expression.

"Sarah," Ethan began, pulling them back on track and preventing any discussion of his uncharacteristic behavior. "Can you give us a description of the man impersonating the guard?"

Nodding, Sarah said, "He was shorter than you…" She gestured toward Ethan and continued, "By a few inches. He had long, black hair tied back in a ponytail, an olive complexion and dark eyes. I don't know exactly what color."

"What was he wearing?" Bella asked.

"A green suit, matching pants and jacket, and a white shirt that was open at the neck, and no tie," Sarah replied.

"Anything else?" said Owen. "Accents? Birthmarks? Tattoos?"

"Accents?" Sarah said thoughtfully. "Just American, really. The same as yours. I think he had a tattoo on his neck…" She paused, thinking. "Maybe an eagle on the world?"

"The world?" Owen asked, confused.

"Planet Earth," Sarah clarified.

Ethan startled at the possibilities floating across his mind. *Semper Fidelis. The Marines.*

"Ethan, what does that mean?" Sarah said.

Ethan blanked his expression in an attempt to reassure her but, immediately, her expression clouded. "Don't do that, Ethan," she said. "Don't treat me like some fragile female. I am a grown adult. I can handle a little bad information."

Ethan wasn't certain why he answered her but he did. "That could be a Marine Corps tatt," he said.

"The Marines?" Sarah said, clearly stunned by that information. "What does that mean?"

"I don't know. Sarah, I really don't know at this point," he said. "Thank you for the lemonade."

Clearly displeased at being so summarily dismissed, she narrowed her eyes at him, the grim line of her mouth relaxing as she approached her children.

"How did you hear about this?" Ethan asked Owen and Bella.

"You're still our star witness, remember?" Bella said, continuing with a challenge in her voice, "Suspended officer or not. And our team is still assigned to Vakh."

Ethan nodded once, accepting the loyalty behind her words. "What now?"

"We find you all a new safe house across the city and we put on a new security detail. Then we track down Borz Vakh," Bella said. "How connected can a Chechen rebel be?"

"Connected enough to find us here."

CHAPTER 5

Disoriented at first by the unfamiliar environment, Sarah lay quietly trying to discover what had roused her from sleep. They were in a new safe house across the city in a much nicer neighborhood; a small bungalow squeezed between two three-story monstrosities, complete with a country kitchen, lounge, two small bedrooms and a three piece washroom.

The noise filtered into her awareness again from the bedroom next door. *It sounds like pleading.* Ethan was clearly tormented by his past...or his present, she wasn't certain. Rolling over, she checked that the boys were still asleep snuggled amongst the covers, and pulled on her bathrobe. Listening at the door, she heard the clear sounds of torment coming from inside Ethan's bedroom. On the other nights, he had calmed after a few minutes but tonight the pleading continued.

Knocking lightly on his bedroom door, Sarah opened it slowly when she received no response. It was too dark to see anything but she could hear the struggle as his body moved amongst the covers.

"Ethan," she whispered. "Are you okay?" No response. She tiptoed over to his bedside and turned the lamp on low, seeing his battered body tangled in the covers, his blonde hair drenched in perspiration. He was clearly asleep and Sarah experienced a moment of indecision which ended when he began to toss again.

"No. Don't. Please, don't go. Please!" he cried and Sarah's heart clenched at the pitiable voice from the usually strong and self-controlled man.

"Ethan, it's okay. You're safe. Ethan, you're safe," she reassured him, keeping her voice firm and calm.

He stilled and his eyes opened, looking straight up and then over toward Sarah.

"What are you doing?" he asked gruffly.

"You were having a nightmare," she said.

"Sorry," he said. It sounded like an automatic response.

"Why would you apologize for having a nightmare?" she asked, curious.

"For waking you," he clarified.

"You wake me every night but you usually settle back to sleep on your own. Tonight you didn't," she said.

His eyes widened in surprise as she spoke. "Sorry. It…it happens quite a lot." This time his voice was softer, gentler.

What kind of life have you led, Ethan Lange? "Would you like some hot cocoa?" she asked aloud.

"No," he said. "Go back to bed."

Sarah laughed. "You really are used to being the boss, aren't you? I'm not going to be able to go back to sleep for a while so I'm going to make a cup of cocoa. Would you like one?"

Ethan studied her for a moment but she couldn't read his expression. "Yes, thank you," he finally said, sitting up, an obviously unwilling groan escaping him.

Realizing that his activities the previous day must have aggravated his injuries, she stepped over to help him. "You're so sore," she said. "Come on and let me help you."

He pushed her hand away. "I don't need anyone, Brigitte."

Pulling back, Sarah said, "Brigitte?"

Ethan corrected, "Sarah."

"You are very stubborn. No wonder Charlie likes you so much," she asked.

He raised his eyes in confusion to her face. "What do you mean?"

"About what? Charlie liking you? I would think it's rather obvious. He takes his books and curls up on the sofa with you several times a day. He doesn't see any of your gruffness. He only sees the kindness you try so hard to keep locked away." Sarah shrugged. It was obvious to her that Charlie liked Ethan. "I can see that you've lead a difficult and, perhaps, dangerous life? But I also see a gentleness in you that I'm not certain you realize that you possess. Charlie doesn't just curl up on the sofa with anyone."

"Teddy?" he inquired, his voice very quiet.

"He's still a little afraid of you. I think he's associated you with the fear of the gallery attack because you grabbed him. I'm sure it was a great shock to him. But he gave you a hug yesterday. That's big. He's a sensitive little fellow but also very forgiving."

Ethan shook his head and she couldn't detect the reason. "You're a wonderful mother," Ethan said, looking up to meet her gaze again.

Flattered by the praise, Sarah responded gratefully, "Thank you. I love being a mother but parenting is hard to do alone."

Ethan finally leveraged his body to the edge of the bed. "Why are you alone?" he asked, reaching out his hand to give her permission to help him. Taking hold, she wrapped her other arm around his shoulders, helping him come forward and off the bed. After the first few steps toward the kitchen, his gait eased and he shook off her help.

"I'm a widow," she said.

"I'm sorry for your loss," Ethan replied automatically. "It must be hard to raise two kids on your own."

"David and I always wanted children, a house full, but it didn't happen as planned. When the doctors told us that children were not going to be an option, we started the process for adoption. We adopted Teddy when he was eleven months old. Then I found I was pregnant and we had our family, smaller than planned but wonderful. And then he just died."

"Just died? What do you mean?" Ethan asked as made his way behind her, finally coming to rest, leaning against the kitchen countertop.

Sarah filled a pot with milk, dumping in a few scoops of cocoa and sugar. "David died of an aneurysm while I was still pregnant with Charlie. He never met him. Neither boy will ever remember their father." Sarah's eyes filled with old emotion. "Sorry," she apologized, sniffing to control the tears. Unexpectedly, she felt a warm hand on her shoulder and she turned to Ethan, allowing his comfort just for a moment. "Thank you," she said, moving away abruptly to retrieve the mugs and setting them on the kitchen counter. *The last thing I want to do is fall to pieces in front of this man.* When she turned again, Ethan was sitting at the table, his face blank of emotion.

Once the mixture heated, she poured some into each mug, added a little cream and brought them over to the table, setting one before Ethan and keeping one. "You know what? I'm hungry. Are you hungry?" she asked, retrieving a few cookies from a package in the cupboard.

Ethan asked, "What brought you here? You're not American."

Smiling lightly at the question, she responded, "No, I'm Canadian. David and I always planned to travel, especially here to Washington DC. So I decided to bring the boys and come and…" She paused, gathering her thoughts. "It's been lovely in some ways and has allowed me to see that life can go on beyond my grief. It's been hard, though, to realize all that the boys will miss experiencing with their father."

"Trust me, having a father isn't always the answer," Ethan said, studying his thumbs as they rested against his mug.

"Are you talking about yourself or your own father?" Sarah said.

"I've never had children. I was married…once…but she didn't want children…and neither did I. My own childhood wasn't exactly idyllic," Ethan said.

"What happened? To your marriage, I mean," Sarah asked quietly, a small feeling of pity mixed with a now familiar wariness pulling at her heart.

"She found someone more interesting; someone willing to be around for her. We've been divorced for ten years," he said.

"I guess that means we've both been abandoned by the ones we love," she said.

Ethan looked up in surprise. "Your husband died. My wife just found a better man." His eyes fell to study his thumbs again.

"Is that where your sadness comes from?" she asked, ducking her head to try and meet his gaze.

Clearly bothered by her question, Sarah watched as he wiped his face clear of expression again. "There's no advantage to being happy. It only leads to disappointment," he said and she wondered if he actually believed that.

Deeply saddened by his words, she felt the urge to wrap him in her arms but she resisted, feeling that he wouldn't welcome that kind of intrusion and feeling totally unwilling to begin the journey down that path. *There's nothing I need from another man, certainly not a man like Ethan Lange.*

"I've, uh, gathered that there's some problem with your job as well. You're an undercover officer or a spy or something, aren't you?"

"Not such a good one if you can tell," he said, his previously blank face clearly revealing his astonishment.

She laughed. "David worked for CSIS, the Canadian Security Intelligence Services. He wasn't a spy himself but some of our friends were. It's easy to interpret the signs when you know what you're looking for. Do you work for the FBI or Homeland Security or something? Have you been suspended? I would assume that it was a set-up because you seem to be a man of integrity except that you act like you deserve to suffer. So I'm guessing you messed up somehow."

Releasing a single burst of disbelief, Ethan said, "You are a remarkable woman. I...can't...ah..." He subsided and quirked his brow in a "oh, well" gesture. "I work undercover with an anti-terrorism initiative."

"Is that what the SWAT guy meant when he called Bella a 'night crawler'?" Sarah said.

"Night crawler?" he quoted, shrugging to show that he didn't know what she meant.

"Night crawler?" she repeated, mimicking him. "The British call their spies 'spooks'." She gestured to show that she had guessed that he was being purposely obtuse.

He finally gave in. "Yes. They call us nightcrawlers. I'm sure you can figure out why."

"Back alleys and cover stories. What did you do, Ethan?" she asked.

"It's common knowledge…been in the newspapers." Ethan cleared his throat. "I let a known terrorist escape in order to save a life. And then he killed a public figure," Ethan said, quickly hiding his misery behind blankness.

"It's a good thing to save a life, Ethan," she said gently.

"I know. It's what I do, don't forget. But—" he began, interrupted by Charlie's sleep voice as he toddled out of the bedroom.

"Mama. Mama."

Sarah picked him up when he approached, giving him a hug and a kiss. Searching the room sleepily, Charlie spotted Ethan and, slipping off his mother's lap, moved around to the big man, tapping his leg and raising his arms. Ethan's hand dropped, it seemed without his permission, to ruffle the little boy's hair but he didn't seem to realize Charlie's desire until Charlie spoke the words.

"Up pease," Charlie said.

Ethan's eyes widened in surprise and he looked over to Sarah, seemingly for her permission. After her nod, Ethan braced his ribs and lifted Charlie onto his lap, tucking him into his elbow. Almost immediately, the little boy's eyes drooped.

"Why would saving a life lead to a suspension?" she asked, returning to their conversation.

"The man I saved was an FBI agent, considered to be able to fend for himself," Ethan said.

"I still don't understand," she said.

"The agent was my ex-wife's husband," he said.

"Ahhh. I would have thought it was more suspicious if you'd let him die. How did your ex-wife react when she realized what you had done for her?" Sarah said.

"She despised me for it; said it was unfair of me to make her husband responsible for another person's death," he said.

"I'm sorry," Sarah said, moved by his plight.

"You've nothing to be sorry for," he replied automatically.

"Were you—are you still in love with her?" Sarah asked.

Ethan snorted and Charlie stirred on his lap. "Love is not an option in my line of work. I learned that early on." *It was Brigitte herself who taught me, in fact. Or maybe it happened before that.*

"Wait a minute. The Chechen fellow, Borz Vakh? He's the terrorist you released, isn't he? That's how he recognized you at the art gallery," Sarah said

"I'm going back to bed. Thanks for the cocoa," he replied, his voice flat and expressionless again. Standing abruptly, flinching at the jolt from his protesting ribs, Ethan thrust Charlie into her arms and moved away to his bedroom.

Sarah carried Charlie back to bed, soon drifting off to sleep herself.

Lying in bed unable to sleep, Ethan remembered the warmth of Charlie's little body tucked against his side. *When was the last time someone chose my company, someone who wasn't required to by work? Is Sarah right? Does little Charlie really like me?* Ethan sighed morosely. Perhaps the boy was just attaching himself to the only male figure in his life regardless of their fitness for any kind of paternal role.

That didn't mean that he didn't wish it were true. *What would it actually feel like to give love and to be loved in return?* Brigitte had made it quite clear that she'd never really loved him. Three weeks after he'd begun with the FBI, they'd gone on a few dates, attending the stag-and-doe of a friend of hers, hitting it off and then deciding to get married. Within hours of the abruptly organized wedding, it was clear to Brigitte, at least, that the relationship was a mistake. Ethan had been willing to try to make it work but three months later, Brigitte had found her "one true love", Ethan's fellow FBI agent, Werner Smith, and Ethan had been unwilling to interfere, knowing it was already too late anyway.

"Ethan, I care for you, that's obvious to anyone, I think," Brigitte had said. "But I just can't be with you, could never be with you. You bury your heart so deeply that no one can ever reach it. I can't do it, Ethan. You really are just your job and nothing else. You're a shell of a man," she'd said.

After years of being nothing but a disappointment to his father, less intelligent than his older brother, Ryan, and less athletic than his younger brother, Steve, Ethan couldn't see himself through any other lens. So when the opportunity to join the CAUDO Project, a clandestine counter-terrorism team set up as a cooperative venture between the FBI and Homeland Security, Ethan leaped.

And then Borz Vakh had held Werner at gunpoint during his escape after a bungled attempt to bomb the off-site hearings of the Bureau of Indian Affairs task force. Ethan had allowed Vakh's escape to save Brigitte's husband. *What else could I do? I'd caused Brige enough pain. I owed it to her. Did I think that she would love me for it?*

Brigitte's response had been scathing. "You had no right to do that, Ethan, to make Werner responsible for the death of a public figure. You have no feelings, do you?" she'd said, still able to make his chest burn ten years after their impulsive marriage and subsequent divorce.

Ethan had already known that he was unlovable. He really hadn't needed the reminder.

CHAPTER 6

Sarah awoke when Charlie's hand slapped across her face. Brushing his pale blonde hair back from his brow, she watched him sleep, seeing his father in the shape of his face, the color of his hair, the restless pattern of his sleep. He was the wiggliest sleeper, tossing and turning all night, and then spending hours with his arms and legs flung wide across the bed. *Wait a minute. Didn't I put Teddy beside me and Charlie against the wall? Where's Teddy?*

Sarah rolled out of bed, checking the floor, the closet. No Teddy. She tiptoed into the hall, checking the washroom and finding it empty.

"Teddy," she whispered and then again more loudly, "Teddy."

With nowhere else to check in the little bungalow, Sarah knocked on Ethan's bedroom door.

"Come," Ethan said.

Pushing the door open cautiously, she spotted Ethan crouching by the window clad in a t-shirt and long pyjama pants. "Ethan, have you seen Teddy? I can't find him," she said.

"He's in here," Ethan said. "He wandered in half-asleep and crawled into bed."

"Really?" Sarah released a quiet laugh of surprise, smothering the sound quickly with her hand so as not to awaken her son. "I'll move him for you," she said as she stepped toward the bed.

"Just leave him," Ethan said. "He's fine."

Sarah sat down on the floor beside Ethan, resting her back against the wall. "What's going on? Did Teddy kick you out of bed?"

"No. I've been up for a while," he said, turning to her. "Teddy's fine. Why don't you go back to bed?"

"Mama. Mama!" Charlie called from the hallway.

"Charlie, Mama's here," she said, picking him up as he sleepily wandered into her arms.

"You can put him with Teddy, Sarah," Ethan said.

Shrugging, Sarah slipped Charlie onto the bed beside his brother and then sat on the floor again.

"What—" Sarah began but Charlie's reappearance interrupted her words. Reaching up, he pulled down on Ethan's shoulder, the unexpected weight unbalancing the man, forcing him to catch himself on the tips of his fingers and putting himself at the perfect height for a good-night kiss.

"Night-night Eefan," Charlie said, kissed him on the cheek and then returned to bed, pulling the covers up and rolling toward Teddy's back.

Sarah watched Ethan's face closely in the light of the full moon, noting the bewilderment in his eyes as he slipped from a three point crouch to his knees. Giving his head a small shake, he resumed his intense staring out the window. A sudden movement from the bushes pulled Sarah's attention away from Ethan to the possible reason for his vigil.

Placing a silencing finger to his lips, he drew his handgun from the floor beside him. "There's someone out there, someone who's been there for over an hour," he whispered.

"Won't the guards take care of it?" she asked.

"The *officers*," he clarified.

"Whatever." She waved away his comment. "Won't they take care of the prowler?"

"They haven't yet," Ethan said.

"You don't really trust these *officers*, do you?" she said. "Do they work with you?"

"Nope. Real FBI. And I don't trust anybody." Ethan turned to her. "Why don't you just go to bed? I'll take care of things."

"You expect me to sleep when I know there's a burglar or a terrorist right outside my window? Seriously?" she said, winging her eyebrows. "Tell me what I can do."

He seemed to study her for a moment in the moonlight before responding. "Coffee?"

Laughing lightly, she said, "That is just an excuse to get me out of here. You don't look in any more need of caffeine than I feel."

"True," he said and she was certain that she saw a ghost of a smile cross his lips. "Stay close." Looking out the window again first, he then turned back to her. "If anything happens, I want you to take the boys into the washroom and lock the door. There's no window in there."

"All right," she said.

They sat together in silence for a time but once Ethan returned his handgun to the floor beside him, she realized the immediate threat was postponed and decided that it was her turn for an interrogation, to better know this man who was worming his way into the heart of her youngest son.

"Ethan, tell me about your family," she said.

"I have two brothers," he replied simply.

"A mother and a father? Yes, I guessed that. What is your mother like?" she said.

Glancing aside at her, he replied slowly, "I don't remember. She died when I was seven."

"I'm sorry." Reaching out, she stroked his arm, automatically lending sympathy. "You must remember something."

Sighing, he reluctantly responded, "She was like you, full of love and life and energy."

Surprised, Sarah responded, "Is that how you see me?"

Turning his head, he met her gaze. "Yes."

"Thank you," she said, humbled by his words. "How did your mother die?"

"Car accident. On the way back from the emergency room with me. Stitches. Drunk driver." Ethan's words came out in a flurry of vocabulary.

"Oh, Ethan, I'm so sorry," Sarah said.

"If I hadn't taken a nose dive from my headboard, we wouldn't have been out in the middle of the night," he said and her mother's heart mourned for him.

"But you must know that it wasn't your fault," she said. "Ethan, you don't blame yourself, do you?"

"My father did. Still does." Where she heard a hint of bitterness, his next words were spoken without bile. "You don't need to look at me with such pity. I'm fine," he said in a matter of fact tone. "I told you before. Happiness only leads to disappointment. If you don't expect anything from life, it usually delivers."

"I happen to expect quite a lot from life," she said. "I have found that even in the deepest despair, God can bring us joy. Without God...well, I guess I'd be lost to despair."

"Despair is an okay neighborhood," he replied.

Sadly, Sarah sighed. "Well, at least now I understand why you shut your heart away."

He didn't respond and she couldn't read his expression. When she reached out to touch him, he grabbed her hand, stilling her movements, instructing her tersely to, "Shhh!"

The beam from a flashlight flickered across the window and two muffled voices traveled to her ears: the creepers.

"There was two guys before but now I don't see no one," said creeper number one, his voice gruff and rumbling.

"Back door's the best way in," said creeper two, stopping to hack and cough before moving away.

Pulling Sarah by the arm, Ethan gestured for her to accompany him to the bedroom door where he whispered directly into her ear, his breath warm on her cheek.

"Stay here," he said. "I'm going to give them a little surprise."

"Be careful. Please," she said.

Nodding, he moved into the hallway toward the back door as Sarah watched from the doorway. Sarah watched in rising dread as the door opened slowly revealing a tattered sneaker. Ethan pushed but the door rebounded. The creeper's fist curved around to grapple with the unseen resistance. Grabbing the doorknob, Ethan jerked it toward him this time, propelling creeper one into the room, the steel pipe in his hand continuing the arc of acceleration to land across Ethan's back, jarring his ribs and wringing a gasp of pain from him. When the pipe swung again, Ethan was ready, blocking it with his forearm and returning the blow, smashing the barrel of his Glock against the creeper's forehead. Sarah watched the slow motion roll of the creeper's eyes back into his head and his collapse on the floor of the hallway. Grasping the creeper's shirt, Ethan dragged him into the kitchen, pinning him to the floor with his knee.

Reaching up, Ethan grabbed a kitchen towel off the counter. Bending to tie the man's wrists, Ethan missed the second intruder who'd crawled in through the kitchen window. Quickly crossing the space, creeper two raised a baseball bat. Instinctively, Sarah reacted, crossing the space at full speed. Pushing Ethan out of the way just in time, the bat missed him but caught her with a glancing blow. Dazed, she fell to the floor beside Ethan. Ethan dispatched her attacker with two punches to the face.

Kneeling on creeper one to pin him to the floor, Ethan trained his gun on creeper two and then contacted the FBI security officers. Returning from the coffee shop where they had retreated, the officers took the creepers into custody.

And then Ethan was beside her, helping her up, asking her again and again if she was okay. She nodded and then shook her head, flinching when he grasped her by the shoulders. Gently, he moved her pyjama shirt aside to look at her shoulder, clenching his jaw at the bruising he saw.

"What were you thinking?" he asked roughly. "Don't ever do that again. Understand?" He pulled her close, hugging her tightly against him and then abruptly releasing her. After a moment of hesitation, he strode to the front of the house, trying to move away from her, she decided.

Pulling out his cell phone, she heard him talking to someone she assumed was Bella.

"What do you mean? They're nothing but common thieves?" Ethan brushed a hand through his short, blonde hair. "Are we or are we not compromised in this location?" He sighed in what sounded like relief though he looked anything but relieved. "Fine. Keep me informed."

Meeting her gaze briefly across the space, Ethan dropped his eyes quickly, moving around the house to secure every potential portal into their supposed "safe house". Realizing just how much her shoulder was throbbing Sarah retrieved a towel from the washroom and loaded it with ice cubes.

"Sorry. I didn't think. Let me do that." Ethan suddenly appeared at her side, apologizing profusely.

"Ethan. Stop. I'm okay," she said, exasperated by his odd response.

"Okay? You took that hit for me. I shouldn't—you couldn't—I don't—"

Covering his mouth with her hand, she stopped his speech. "I'm okay," she repeated kindly, not able to resist the urge to brush her thumb across his whiskery cheek, feeling his sharp intake of breath. His brilliant blue eyes were riveted on her deep browns and a frisson buzzed between them. *Why am I doing this? I don't need love in my life. Love is complicated. I'm alone with the boys. And we're fine.*

Slowly raising his hand, Ethan removed her palm from his mouth, pressing it against his chest where she felt the strong rhythm of his heart. Her eyes rose again to his slightly parted lips. Inexplicably, the distance between them decreased and Ethan's hand was suddenly tangled in her hair.

"I'm sorry," he whispered, resting his forehead against hers.

"Don't," she said, pulling back, not certain herself what she meant.

Abruptly, he spun away, leaving her cold. "Leave the boys. I'll sleep on the sofa," he called over his shoulder.

Sarah gathered up the ice-filled towel and went to bed.

CHAPTER 7

SPLASH! Ethan startled awake, groaning at the pull on his ribs caused by the quick reflexive movement.

"Teddy, that is not funny! Go and find something to do!"

Ethan groaned loudly at the effort to rise from the sofa, quite certain that he couldn't be heard over the commotion from the washroom. Dressing first in his vacated bedroom, he made his way to the source of the noise.

"Teddy!" Sarah said. Her voice was stern and very *mommy'ish*. Ethan watched as the little boy tossed toy dinosaurs over his mother's crouching form and into the bathtub causing a squeal of laughter to erupt from the occupant of the tub. "Charles Henry, sit down!" Ethan heard a sharp smack and Charlie protested angrily with a scream of indignation. But he sat.

"Don't do that!" Ethan rebuked Sarah, stepping forward into the room. "There's no need to hit him."

Clearly annoyed by the intrusion, Sarah said, biting out the words, "I didn't '*hit*' him. I applied a slight sting to his hindquarters to add emotion to the lesson."

"If you can't manage to handle—"

Standing abruptly, Sarah spun to face him, her eyes rimmed in exhaustion, hair messy and the front of her wet denim shirt pulled out of her jeans and clinging to her.

"How dare you?" Shoving him with both hands, she forced him back and slammed the door in his face.

Shocked, he stared at the door until he felt a tug on his hand. Looking down he met Teddy's serious gray eyes.

"I got in trouble, too. Wanna play *Go Fish*?" Teddy asked. Ethan felt too stunned to respond at first. Teddy continued, "Mommy's mad 'cause Charlie poured a whole bottle o' ketchup on the floor and then made a *huge*," Teddy spread his arms wide, "picture of a elephant. He likes to finger paint."

"Show me," Ethan said, taking a firmer grip on Teddy's hand as the boy led him to the kitchen. Ethan laughed once and then released a loud guffaw, clutching his ribs to support his hilarity. Teddy laughed with him. "It *is* a very good elephant," Ethan said.

"Uh huh," Teddy replied, still giggling happily.

"Where was Mommy?" Ethan said.

"She aksed us to play quiet at the table 'cause you were sleepin' an' she needed a' get dressed but it was bo~or~ing so I built a fort," Teddy said. Ethan looked over to see every pillow, cushion, towel and blanket in the little house heaped in a mass behind the sofa. "Charlie got bored too so he went to get a snack."

"I suppose we should clean it up," Ethan said.

Teddy agreed reluctantly. "I s'pose."

Together, boy and man mopped and wiped the floor so that, by the time Sarah emerged with a dripping Charlie, Teddy and Ethan were adding the sofa cushions to the pile of *fort*.

"Teddy, could you please bring me a towel from your fort?" Sarah asked, her voice relaxed and calm again.

"Sure, Mommy," Teddy replied, hopping over and retrieving a kitchen towel for his mother.

She held out the tiny cloth between her thumb and index finger, a grin bursting across her face chased by a laugh of joy. "Thank you, Teddy David. Could I perhaps have a slightly larger one?" Teddy shrugged and skipped back to the fort.

Charlie wiggled in her arms and Sarah turned to him. "Want to find your own towel?" she asked and the boy nodded. "Will you get dressed when I tell you to?" she said, one eyebrow raised. Charlie nodded again and she put him on the floor, watching with a smile as he ran over and jumped into the pile of cushions. Ethan noticed there was no redness on his hip. Sarah was right. She hadn't marked him.

"Uh—" Ethan began.

Turning to him, Sarah said, "I'm sorry I yelled at you. I was just so frustrated. Charlie wouldn't sit and Teddy kept intruding, poking me and tossing things into the tub. They're going stir-crazy being held indoors so long. Normally, we spend several hours a day outside."

"I'm, uh, sorry to have interfered," Ethan mumbled.

"I would never harm my children, Ethan, no matter how frustrated I felt," she said firmly.

"Of course not," he replied sincerely. "Would you like some scrambled eggs?" He wasn't sure why, but he didn't want to risk an argument with Sarah. Not today, anyway. Not after she'd saved him last night.

"Actually, we've had our breakfast. I would prefer a cup of coffee. Do we still have any? When do the guards bring our next shipment of groceries?" she said.

"This isn't a prison, Sarah," he said.

"Ethan!" Sarah stopped at the edge of the kitchen, crying out and startling him. "Did you clean this up?" she said with wonder in her eyes. At his affirmative, she took a step toward him and wrapped him in a warm hug before he could decide on a course of action to prevent such a response. "Thank you," she said. "I haven't had anyone to help me in a long time. I'll, uh, be right back." He saw the glimmer of tears in her eyes as she fled to the washroom. She'd been dry-eyed through two attacks on her life yet a small act of kindness brought her to tears. Sarah was like no one Ethan had ever known before.

After pouring some coffee, Ethan leaned back against the counter to watch the little clothed and naked bodies flying around the room, jumping, running and giggling. An unexpected grin pulled his face into a smile that somehow warmed him through and through.

After lunch, Sarah put the boys in front of the television and sighed into a chair at the kitchen table. *One more task and then I can rest.*

"Ethan," she began, waiting until he lowered his newspaper before continuing. "I was supposed to change the dressing on your stitches yesterday and I forgot. We'd better do it now."

Shrugging, he said, "Don't worry about it."

"Are you going to be difficult?" Sarah said, sighing. "Because, frankly, I would rather you just manned-up and got it over with."

"And if I refuse," Ethan said, narrowing his eyes.

Putting on her best *mommy* face, the *do-it-or-face-the-consequences* expression, Sarah said, "You may think you're too old to be—"

"I give," he said, chuckling as he raised his hands in surrender. "You are quite fierce when you're angry. You know that, don't you?"

She hadn't expected humor from him. He was always so serious and intense. Releasing her own tension, she grinned in return, retrieving the bandages and ointment. Ethan sat very still as she slowly peeled away the gauze on his chin and over his eyebrow. One of the stitches was caught in the fabric and as Sarah moved in closer to deal with it, she caught herself inhaling the spicy scent that Ethan always seemed to emit. Finally noticing his stillness, she glanced down to see his eyes riveted on her face.

"Sorry," he mumbled, dropping his gaze.

Unsettled by his response to her proximity, she said, "Don't apologize. I'm sure...it's just the tension of the situation...never mind." Abruptly, she scooped up the medicaments and turned away. "We need to leave the bandage off for a few hours but we should cover it again before bed—uh, slee—tonight."

Feeling an unusual contentment, Ethan returned to the newspaper as Sarah returned to Charlie. He could hear her voice undulating with the story she read to the little boy.

Teddy's roars rang out from the bedroom where he played out a prehistoric drama with his dinosaurs.

"Mommy!" Teddy's voice rang out from the bedroom. "Mommy." Appearing at the bedroom door, he shrank back when he spotted Ethan. "Hi," he said, offering a tentative wave.

"Hi, Teddy," Ethan replied. The boy was still cautious around him. "Do you need something?"

His voice was very soft as he replied, "I wanted t'know if Mommy wanted t'play *Go Fish*."

"Charlie, don't!" Sarah's voice came from the other room followed by a resounding crash.

"Uh oh," Ethan said. "Charlie's in for it now."

Giving Ethan a tremulous grin, Teddy replied, "Yup. I guess Mommy won't play."

Sarah's voice rang out again. "Charles Henry, whatever gave you the notion that this was a good idea? Go in the other room until I clean this up and then we're going to have a chat," Sarah said but it didn't sound like any kind of chat that Ethan would want to participate in. "Now!" she said and soon Charlie scampered into the kitchen. He ran directly to Ethan, arms outstretched, tears falling down his cheeks. Ethan knew a moment of paralyzed panic which Charlie seemed to interpret as acceptance because he climbed right into Ethan's lap, wrapped his little boy arms tightly around Ethan's neck and buried his face against Ethan's shirt. Instinctively, Ethan closed his arms around the boy.

Teddy walked over and patted Charlie's back. "Wanna play *Go Fish*, Charlie?" he said and Ethan assumed that was Teddy's idea of consolation.

Hiccupping, Charlie replied, "Okey-*hic*-dokey," and then wiped his runny nose on the shoulder of Ethan's shirt. "Wanna pay, Eefan?" Charlie said, his teary gaze meeting Ethan's.

"Sure. Why not?" Ethan said. "You'll have to teach me how to play, though."

Teddy became serious for a moment and then a shy smile spread across his face. "Really?" he said.

"Sure," Ethan replied, turning to Teddy and his wonder-filled eyes.

"Okay," Teddy said, running into the bedroom to retrieve his playing cards.

Soon Ethan was laughing and truly enjoying himself for the first time in what felt like years.

"Ethan," Teddy admonished. "You can't do that. That's cheating!"

"Says who?" Ethan said.

"Mommy says," Teddy replied. "Want me to go ask her?"

"Fine. You win. I'll put it back," Ethan offered in mock defeat.

"Are you scared of mommy?" Teddy asked in his serious voice as Charlie turned on Ethan's lap to look up at his face, clearly wondering the same thing.

Ethan chuckled. "Should I be do you think?"

"Nah. Mommy's the greatest!" Teddy's voice rang with assurance.

"Charlie," Sarah called as she entered the kitchen.

"Me hewe Eefan," Charlie replied.

And Ethan knew a moment of doubt when he saw Sarah's frown. "He was crying," Ethan said, immediately on the defensive. "I thought—sorry—should I have—"

Sarah smiled happily at him. "No, you did the perfect thing. Thank you." Stepping over, she kissed Ethan lightly on the temple as she ruffled Charlie's hair, bringing a giggle from the boy. "He especially is going stir-crazy being kept indoors so much," she said. "Thank you."

Embarrassment and pleasure warred within Ethan and he struggled to keep a blush from rising up his neck.

"I should put clean bandages on your stitches now," she said and he nodded.

As Sarah applied the antibacterial ointment and fresh bandages, Ethan kept his mind on the color of the walls and the grain in the wood table and anything but how good she smelled and how cool her fingers felt against his face as she gently cared for him. But the pleasant tension coiling within him was released when a knock sounded on the door. Ethan shot out of his chair, startling Sarah. Teddy's arm shot out and he grasped a fistful of Sarah's shirt, a look of alarm on his face. But Charlie slapped Ethan on the leg, halting his retreat. Ethan looked down at the little boy's pale blue eyes.

"New toys?" Charlie asked.

"I don't know, pal," Ethan replied, ruffling the boy's hair. "Come and see."

Requesting the password, Ethan looked through the peephole and then released the locks. Stepping back to open the door, he took Charlie by the hand to move him out of the way.

"Brigitte," Ethan said and his voice was tight even to his own ears. "Come in."

Charlie gripped Ethan's hand and flattened himself against his leg.

"New toys?" Charlie whispered and Ethan bent down to hear the words.

Smiling softly at the boy, Ethan straightened to speak with Brigitte. "He would like to know if you have any toys."

Brigitte seemed flustered by the question, her gaze flicking between the boy and the man. "N-no, sorry," she said.

Charlie's eyes fell so Ethan suggested he go play with Teddy.

"Okay!" Charlie answered running back to the kitchen.

"Have a seat, Brige." Ethan gestured to the sofa. Conversations with Brigitte always left him cold and, in contrast to the warmth he'd just experienced playing with Sarah's little boys, Ethan wanted this over with as quickly as possible. "Would like some coffee or anything?"

"No, thank you, Ethan. I need to speak with you," Brigitte said. Her voice was so familiar to him and yet lacking in any enthusiasm or warmth. Had it always been this way? Sarah's voice was always warm and comforting, in spite of the fact that the sum total of their relationship had occurred because of the mortal danger he'd exposed her to in his attempt to save her sons from a mercenary cum terrorist. Ethan swallowed a morose sigh and sat at the other end of the sofa.

"What did you think you were doing?" Brigitte asked, rebuking him. For what? Putting his life on the line to save Teddy and Charlie? And Sarah?

"I couldn't let the villains hurt the little boys," Ethan said fiercely. He was sick and tired of guilt. Everywhere he went, the people in his life were burying him in guilt. His father, his brothers, his Team Leader, his ex-wife.

Hmphing, Brigitte broke his train of thought. "I've come to tell you that the enquiry begins the day after tomorrow. I've contacted your lawyer and provided him with the necessary documents. You will be retrieved in the morning and taken to the local FBI Headquarters," Brigitte said. Her voice was cold and clinical. *Had there ever been anything like love between them?*

Brigitte rose and then sat abruptly. "Why did you do it, Ethan? How am I—how is he meant to hold his head up high?" Her voice was warming to anger now.

Ethan knew she wasn't referring to the gallery incident of a few days ago but to the Vakh decision, the decision he'd made three months ago which had led to his suspension and the upcoming enquiry; the decision Ethan had made to save Werner's life which had allowed a known terrorist to assassinate a senator.

"I've seen enough death, Brigitte," Ethan said. "I could save him so I did. I figured I owed you that at least."

"No one will thank you for this," she said, as though he needed the warning.

Guilt. Self-loathing. These were commonplace in Ethan's self-identity. No matter his intentions, he seemed to always destroy the good things in his life. He had turned the decision around his mind a million ways but he still found no way to satisfy his critics.

Ethan didn't want to have this exhausted conversation which painted his act of mercy as the greatest of villainy.

"Brigitte," Ethan said with more assurance than he'd felt in a long time. "It was my choice to make and I made it. It's done. I can't undo it now."

Slapping her hands on her lap, she rose in obvious frustration. "Werner will be called to testify. They'll think your decision was made because of our former relationship."

The spite in her voice at the mention of their brief marriage cut Ethan. "I assumed as much," he said and then continued wryly, "It doesn't seem to me you'll have any difficulty convincing them that there was nothing between us; that I acted on my own without your knowledge."

"Good-bye, Ethan," Brigitte said curtly. "You never change."

CHAPTER 8

Sarah was frustrated with Ethan's new attitude. Obviously, the lovely, slender brunette had brought bad news the day before, but surely a grown man should be able to control his emotions better than this. He had been gruff and distant, once again closing himself off from the boys. And he'd barely spoken to her. He'd grumbled and snapped...and then it happened.

"Cut it out! Get down from there!" Ethan's angry voice carried through the apartment...and half the neighborhood, she was certain. Sarah rushed to intervene in time to see Teddy run from the room and Charlie dissolve into tears and rush into her soapy, wet arms.

Standing, Ethan paced to the front door without a word of apology. "I'm going out," he said, his voice still angry and gruff.

"Oh, you are, are you?" she replied dryly. "We've been stuck in this safe house as long as you have. Why do you get to leave? And what gives you the right to be so mean?"

Stepping threateningly close to her, Ethan raised his voice over Charlie's sobs, saying hotly, "You've no right to speak to me like that!"

"Exactly what are you going to do to prevent it?" she replied, not in the least bit intimidated. "Grow up, Ethan! Bad things happen. Life sucks sometimes but it doesn't give you the right to take it out on the people who care about you."

Charlie in her arms, she turned on her heel and walked into the bedroom, slamming the door behind her.

Consoling the boys, she learned that Teddy had been crawling up on the back of the sofa and jumping down onto the seat and then onto the floor while he waited for the news to finish on TV. He assured her that Ethan had only told him once to stop before he'd yelled at him. Charlie promised

~ 59 ~

earnestly that he had been playing "quiet…so quiet" with some toys on the coffee table.

Pulling Teddy and Charlie into her arms, she cuddled them close on the bed, saying, "Something is bothering Ethan. I don't know what. I guess we'll have to give him some space for a while. Let's go find something to do."

"I don't want to go out, Mommy," Teddy said, his voice panicked.

"Ethan's not there," she said. "He's gone."

"Did he die like Daddy?" Teddy asked quietly.

Sarah's heart clenched for her poor little son. "No, sweetheart. He just went for a walk to get rid of his grumpies. Come on. There must be something we can do that we haven't already done sixty times." Sarah picked them both up and carried them to the kitchen, pulling out a bag of dry pasta and dumping it into a large mixing bowl. She pulled out ten of the noodles, coloring them with markers and hiding them in the mixture. "Let's see how long it takes us to find the red ones," she suggested and the boys dug in, soon lost in the fun of playing in the pasta. They retrieved a few cars and blocks to add to the adventure.

Sarah sat by them at the table, her Bible open before her, feeling very sad. *Why on earth am I upset by this? Just because it took a few days to see the real man doesn't mean I wasn't an idiot for thinking Ethan was anything special. Was that a double negative? Oh, brother! I don't need a man in my life. David is gone and it's just me and the boys. That's the best way, right Father? I have to protect my children. Romance just complicates things.*

Sighing to release some of her grief, Sarah flipped to Psalm 46, "God is our refuge and strength a very present help in trouble." Breathing in the peace and comfort brought by the words of the promise, Sarah prayed…*Thank you, Father.*

Once the pasta lost its charm, they built a fort under the kitchen table and then Sarah put the boys in the bathtub for a *just for fun bath*, no washing required.

Ethan didn't return until night had firmly fallen. Teddy shot into the bedroom as soon as Ethan entered the little bungalow and Charlie didn't come running but stayed in front of the television.

Setting a plastic bag on the kitchen table, Ethan sat heavily on a chair. Sarah ignored him. *He made this mess, he can sort it out.*

"Sarah," he said, his voice husky and quiet. The next time was a little louder. "Sarah, I'm sorry." She turned to him, seeing his entire frame cloaked in misery. He didn't look up to meet her gaze.

"What happened?" She kept her voice even, her anger retreating in sympathy with his misery. But she was not willing to let him off the hook until she understood better his behavior.

"Nothing," he replied.

"Evidently something did happen because you hollered at Teddy, frightening him badly and hurting his feelings," she insisted.

Stiffening as though bracing himself, his voice became more self-assured. "I mean nothing happened that justified my behavior. He was just jumping on the sofa and didn't stop when I told him to." Ethan stopped speaking so Sarah returned to washing the dishes.

"What did you mean when you said I had no right to take it out on the people who care about me? Sarah, I don't know if you've noticed but no one cares about me. My life is a train wreck. I shoot through life hurting everyone I come into contact with," Ethan said, meeting and holding her gaze.

"Oh, Ethan," she replied, sympathy driving her to his side. "You have been a big jerk today but one loss of temper doesn't qualify you as a train wreck. Mistakes can be fixed."

"Not all mistakes," he said. He seemed unable to look away and she couldn't tell whether he was waiting to be condemned or desperately hoping for forgiveness.

"I suppose you must be right," she said. "But this mistake can be." She moved closer to lean against the table beside him.

"What do I do?" he asked, still watching her closely.

"You need to apologize to Teddy. You really scared him, Ethan. He was just beginning to trust you and you treated him very badly."

"Why would he forgive me?" Ethan said, brushing his fingers through his short hair.

"Because he cares about you and Charlie cares about you," she said.

"And you?" he said. Sarah shifted away from him but he wrapped his arm across her waist, stopping her. "Tell me," he said. "The truth. All I want is the truth."

She met his eyes again but she couldn't read anything from the hidden depths. "I, uh, care about you, too," she said, quickly adding, "But I'm not very happy with you at the moment. Apologizing does take you some way toward making things right, though."

Nodding slowly, he pulled her close, resting his head against her, holding her tightly around the waist. Hesitating for a moment, she then wrapped her arms around his shoulders, stroking his hair in comfort, enjoying the soft feel of it. He released her just as abruptly.

"I had no right to do that," he mumbled.

Patting his shoulder in comfort, she sat quietly across the table from him. After a time, he blew out a sigh. "What do I say to him?" he asked.

"Apologize to him. Explain—in four year old terms, of course—and try to do better. He's very sensitive so it will take some time for him to trust you again. But, Ethan, this is not an unfixable situation." She moved back into the kitchen, putting away the plates and glasses.

Ethan nodded. There was a determined expression on his face. "I stopped and bought some new toys and a couple of books. I also bought you some coffee. It's

Ethiopian…supposed to be very good. I've also arranged for you and the boys to go out once a day from now on."

His thoughtfulness brought a smile to her face. "Thank you. It will be nice to get out of here," she said. "I'll let you give the toys to the children."

He nodded again and knocked on the bedroom door. A tiny "come in" followed.

Sarah hugged her arms across her chest, wishing she could hear what was being said. After a time, Teddy emerged carried on Ethan's back and she wondered how the poor man was managing with his battered ribs. Charlie raced over.

"Eefan?" Charlie said. Ethan looked down at Charlie. "Gumpies gone?"

Ethan turned his head to meet Teddy's gaze over his shoulder. "What does he mean?"

Teddy answered quietly, "Mommy said you went for a walk to get your grumpies out."

"Yes. My grumpies are gone," Ethan said. "Sorry, guys."

Teddy kissed Ethan loudly on the ear, making Sarah smile.

"I bought some new toys," Ethan said with a lopsided grin on his face.

"Toys! Toys!" the boys cried together.

Sarah lifted Teddy off Ethan's back and watched as Ethan took out two new dinosaurs, a set of blocks and two books, one about a car and one about a horse. He produced the packet of coffee and gave it to Sarah, wrapping his arms around her in a hug. Eventually she returned it, her mind buzzing from the warmth and care of his touch.

"Thank you, for a second chance," he murmured in her ear, the sensation causing her heart to accelerate.

Breathlessly unable to respond, she gave him an extra squeeze, careful of his ribs.

Ethan spent the next hour playing with the boys, finding that it helped to keep his mind off the upcoming enquiry. Sarah kept her distance physically but she kept a close watch on him, never letting him out of her sight. *Trust is something that must be earned and re-earned,* Ethan reminded himself.

Once the boys were abed, Sarah reappeared and Ethan offered her a coffee, unexpectedly warmed by her friendly acceptance.

Settling at the table across from him, she said, "The woman who arrived today, was that your ex-wife? Is that what made you so cranky?"

"Cranky?" Ethan replied indignantly.

Sarah chuckled at his response and he caught himself smiling along with her. "Yes. That's Brigitte," he said.

"What did she come to tell you?" Sarah asked.

"The enquiry into my conduct begins tomorrow morning," he replied.

"What will happen?" she said.

Frowning, Ethan replied, bitterly, "They're going to tear my career to shreds, and then me. None of the good I've done will matter, only their current displeasure."

"What are your options?" she said.

Shrugging, he considered her question. "I could resign in disgrace and then they might leave me alone. I could fight and, perhaps, win my job back. I could be demoted or even go to prison."

"Prison?" she said, her brows furrowed. "Why not just resign? How can prison be preferable to that?"

"Do you know the funny thing?" he said, though *funny* wasn't exactly how it had felt at the time. "I tried to resign a few months ago but my Team Leader, Jack Dietrich, convinced me to stay; said I was the born to live undercover." Ethan lifted his head to meet her gaze rancorously. "What does it say about me if my Team Leader thinks I'm best fit to spend my days with the scum of the earth and my ex-wife tells me that I am my job?"

"Several years ago, David and I went through a very difficult time," Sarah said. Ethan leaned forward, brows furrowed, confused by the topic shift. "We were having trouble getting pregnant and the medical investigation concluded that it was David's issue. He was deeply affected by that conclusion, becoming erratic at home and at work to the point where he was formally reprimanded for unprofessional behavior. After that, I can tell you, I'd had enough, and insisted he sort himself out. During the argument that followed, he broke down and confessed that he was terrified that I would leave him. He asked me if I wanted a divorce so that I could have children with someone else." She stopped for a moment and Ethan could see the memories flitting across her mind.

"What did you say?" Ethan asked.

"David was more than just a seed donor," she replied. "He was my husband, my lover and my friend. He was a son, an uncle, a nephew, a brother. He was so much more than his ability to reproduce."

"What are you telling me?" Ethan said.

"You are more than your job," she said. "I'm sure that you are very good at what you do but that is not all there is to Ethan Lange. You are more than you think you are." Ethan's eyebrows arched at her words. "What will be accomplished by going to prison?" she asked. "What purpose would be served by falling on your sword?"

"Perhaps I don't feel it's worth fighting," he said, watching her closely.

Without warning, Sarah pushed back from the table, spilling the contents of her coffee cup. "I think that's very selfish of you!" she said, gasping in surprise when Ethan pulled her around to face him.

"Why?" he asked, studying her eyes for the answer he suddenly needed desperately. "Why?"

"Let go of me, now," she said, her voice low and threatening.

Ethan released her, dropping his hands to his sides.

Softly, she said, avoiding his gaze, "Because Teddy and Charlie would miss you."

"And you," he said, tilting her chin up and lowering his mouth to meet hers in the briefest tender touch. He pulled back to see her reaction.

"I'm not looking for love, Ethan. It hurts too much when you lose it," she said, her voice shaky and low. "It would be too complicated to let someone into our lives in that way. I can't. I don't want to. Don't," she said and then she fled into her bedroom, closing him out.

CHAPTER 9

T he next morning, shortly after the boys had finished their breakfasts, Ethan emerged wearing an immaculate charcoal gray suit. He looked devastatingly handsome except for the fact that his face was devoid of all emotion. Responding dully to the boys' greetings emotionlessly, he settled at the table with the newspaper and a cup of coffee. Sarah took pity on him, understanding now how nervous he was about the enquiry, and placed her breakfast before him. Then she made a new one for herself.

Before he'd even finished the eggs and bacon, two bulky, black-suited individuals arrived to escort him away. Pausing at the door, Ethan returned to kiss the tops of the boys' heads, raising his eyes only briefly to Sarah; long enough for her to catch a glimpse of the mourning in his soul.

Their minders took them to a park across the city for a couple of hours of play followed by a fast food lunch. It was with much lightened hearts that Sarah returned to the safe house with her sons. The boys obviously missed Ethan all day but Sarah was glad for the distance after the intensity of their interaction the previous evening.

At suppertime, Ethan had still not returned and Charlie's persistent questioning was beginning to grate on Sarah's nerves. When a knock finally sounded on the door, the boys ran to greet the man but wandered away droopily when it was Brigitte their mother welcomed, not Ethan.

Sarah invited Brigitte to share a pot of coffee and set out a few cookies on a plate.

"I came to warn you," Brigitte said as though launching an attack.

"About what?" Sarah said, taken aback.

"Ethan is not capable of love. He's no more than a shifting false identity, a husk. You have no idea of the things he's done!" Brigitte said and Sarah wondered who she was trying to convince.

"Oh no? Let me guess. He compartmentalizes his life, keeping a piece of himself safe from the villains he spends his days with? He's put himself in the line of danger time and again? He's sacrificed the love of friends and family to meet the demands of the state?" Sarah said.

Brigitte gasped and sat back in her chair. "You—how did you—it doesn't—"

"Are you in love with Ethan?" Sarah asked. *This*, she needed to know.

"We had a brief infatuation that we unfortunately made official. That's it," Brigitte said.

Sarah had finally figured it out. "You don't even know him, not the real Ethan Lange," Sarah said.

Brigitte straightened, her very posture conveying her indignation. "I have known him for over ten years. I was married to him for three months," Brigitte said. Sarah held her gaze and eventually Brigitte slumped down on the sofa, seeming to shrink for a moment. "Perhaps I preferred the mystery of the man to the reality."

Sarah nodded. "I see." And she did. Brigitte wanted the failure of her marriage to be entirely Ethan's fault. And she worked very hard to make that true, even arriving uninvited at a stranger's door and attempting to incite her against him.

Teddy wandered over. "Mommy, when is Ethan coming home?" He leaned against Sarah's shoulder.

"I don't know, sweetheart," Sarah replied sympathetically.

Teddy pulled her down to whisper in her ear. "Does she know?" he asked, pointing at Brigitte.

Sarah whispered back. "I'll ask her." She turned to Brigitte. "Do you know when Ethan will be back?"

"I believe they've put him under house arrest to prevent flight from prosecution," Brigitte replied, her tone as technical as her words.

"What does that mean...for us?" Sarah asked, bewildered by this information.

"I don't really know. I did notice that your guards were gone," Brigitte said.

"We're not supposed to be here. Ethan was protecting us by placing us in the safe house with him. If he's been removed, they will have removed his security." Apprehension fluttered in Sarah's belly. "Teddy, please get Charlie and go brush your teeth before bed."

"Kay," he said, skipping away.

"Who knows you're here?" Brigitte asked.

"Bella Farini and...uh, Owen...uh, Cullen," Sarah said, working hard to remember the names.

Brigitte pulled out her cell phone, saying, "I'll take care of it." But her call was interrupted by a thump against the door.

Just as Sarah rose to investigate, an explosion ripped across the front porch, the concussion knocking Sarah and Brigitte to the floor. The front window shattered, spraying shards of glass through the air above them. The front door burst into flames, smoke billowing into the living room.

"What happened?! What was that?" Brigitte screeched from her position on the floor.

Sarah was up and running toward the back of the house. "Follow me!" she said.

Racing into the bedroom, she grabbed her cell phone, dialing 911, allowing all of her urgency into her voice. Pausing at the door to the washroom, she forcibly calmed her voice, moving over to the two boys with mouths full of toothpaste, relieving them of their toothbrushes, and praising them for such good tooth-brushing. She took their hands, leading them to the back door. She chattered on about the noisy neighbors and that loud bang as she ignored the shock in their eyes.

Shielding their view from the flaming front door, she kept her voice very calm, calling over her shoulder for Brigitte.

"Brigitte. Come now." Sarah insisted and finally Brigitte walked over, her eyes wide with shock, tremors wracking her body.

"Okay, boys, let's go into the back yard to wait for Ethan," Sarah said.

Teddy and Charlie looked up at her, their fear-filled eyes wide, their faces pale. As she opened the back door, Teddy pulled back.

"I need my dinosaurs," he said, running to the bedroom to retrieve his favorites before she could stop him. As she stepped back to reach for him, gunshots ripped into the door frame, narrowly missing them. They were trapped between bullets and fire!

Shoving the boys into the washroom, Sarah went back to get Brigitte, dragging her along with them. Sarah turned the cold water tap in the bathtub on high and soaked some towels, shoving them along the bottom of the washroom door and then soaking more towels to use on any flames that threatened her children. She waited, battle ready, praying for help.

CHAPTER 10

Meeting his lawyer, Clifton Cameron, on the front steps of FBI Headquarters on Pennsylvania Avenue, Washington DC, disgraced Special Agent Ethan Lange was ushered into a meeting room, empty except for seven chairs in a row behind a long conference table. Two chairs were set in the middle of the space. Feeling like he was stepping before a firing squad, Ethan stood beside his lawyer, waiting impatiently as the men and women who would decide the fate of his career, and possibly his liberty, filed into the room and took up their places behind the long table.

"Be seated," the chair of the disciplinary hearing, the newly promoted Assistant Director Jack Dietrich, Ethan's former Team Leader, commanded. "We are here today to determine whether Agent Ethan Everett Lange shall be found in dereliction of duty, and whether there is sufficient evidence to necessitate criminal charges against him in the case of the murder of Senator Tom Baker. You understand, Mr. Lange, that while you are under the authority of this panel, you remain under oath?"

Ethan nodded. "Yes, sir." *Why did they put Dietrich in charge of the investigation?* Dietrich had come under suspicion within the CAUDO Project eight months ago and Ethan, believing him to be a double agent, had provided evidence against him. Dietrich had been exonerated but the two men had maintained an uneasy truce since then. Ethan had opted to remain on Dietrich's team and, to this point, had no personal complaints against the man aside from a feeling of slime whenever they were together. But surely the man could not be considered impartial.

"On the date in question..." And they proceeded to describe the failed bombing and escape of the Chechen mercenary, Borz Vakh. Quickly, though, the recitation became a listing of every mistake and questionable operational decision Ethan had ever made in his professional career. He began to wonder how one person could be responsible for such chaos and destruction.

Finally released in the late afternoon, Ethan expected to be returned to the safe house, to Sarah. He longed to hear her gentle voice and see her smile which occasionally twinkled mischievously in the corner of her eye. He longed to kiss her again, to feel her compassion for him. He badly wanted to hear Teddy and Charlie call his name, greeting him as though they were happy to see him. Unexpectedly though, the panel determined that given Ethan's reputation as a man who followed initiative above orders, he should be held under house arrest in order to prevent flight from prosecution. His heart plummeted within him. *No Sarah. No Teddy and Charlie.* He gulped. *No protection for the little family!*

"Sir." Ethan interrupted the abrupt exit of the panel, directing his comments at the chairman. "Sir, I need to speak with you."

Dietrich turned reluctantly. "What is it, Agent Lange?" he said caustically.

"There was a second witness to the terror attack by Vakh on the National Gallery. She has been staying with me at the safe house," Ethan said. "We need to provide protection for her and her two children."

Narrowing his eyes thoughtfully, Dietrich flipped open the file before him. "There is no record of a second witness," he said.

Ethan continued, "She followed me to the hospital and therefore her details weren't recorded with the other witnesses."

"All the other witnesses were eliminated, Lange," Dietrich said.

"As I said, she was at the hospital with me, sir," Ethan said, feeling that he was losing the man's attention. "That's why her name wasn't recorded, why she's still alive today."

"If there is no record, there is nothing I can do," Dietrich said, turning to go.

"Please, sir. Just let me pick them up and bring them to my house then. I've sworn to protect them," Ethan said, falling just sort of beseeching the man.

"Your security detail has been removed," Dietrich said. "If they needed protection, you should have informed the proper authorities. Good day." Dietrich turned and walked away.

Ethan started after him, quickly restrained by the guards at the door. Stepping back into the room, the chairman ended the discussion. "Your wings need to be properly clipped, Lange. Get him out of here."

"No. Please. Listen to me," Ethan said, finding himself flattened to the floor, his chest burning. Flanked by FBI agents unknown to him, Ethan was led away in zip cuffs.

"It seems to me you've gotten yourself plunged into the middle of something bigger than you. I'm not saying this simply as you're lawyer, Ethan, but it seems clear to me that someone is out to get you," Cameron said by way of a parting comment.

Ethan was distracted by the real fear he felt, fear for Sarah and Teddy and Charlie. *I have to protect them. God, if you're up there, please get me back to them!*

Confined in the back seat of the government-issue black Ford Explorer, Ethan slumped into his seat as though in defeat.

"Do you think you could loosen the cuffs?" Ethan inquired mournfully. "They're cutting off my circulation."

The guard exchanged a glance with the agent in the front passenger seat who nodded. Producing a pocket knife, he sliced through the plastic, releasing Ethan's hands. Slumping forward, Ethan rested his head in his hands, waiting for just the right moment.

As the car accelerated from a stoplight, Ethan leaned toward the guard's lap to his right, retching loudly as though he was about to do the Technicolor yawn. Surreptitiously, Ethan unclipped his seatbelt.

Shoving him away, the guard reached forward to tap the driver on the shoulder, instructing him to pull over. The position made him vulnerable, exposing his unprotected midriff. Ethan drove his fist into the man's solar plexus, winding him. Following up with a double-fisted punch down on the man's neck, Ethan kicked back at the guard on his other side. Propelling his body over the rear seat into the trunk-space of the Explorer, Ethan pushed the inside latch and rolled out the back of the vehicle. He narrowly missed an untimely demise beneath the wheels of a Subaru.

Gritting his teeth against the pain in his chest, Ethan ran through the traffic, dodging back and forth. Crouching low when he heard, "Freeze" Ethan continued running, the shots sailing over his head. Racing in through the open door of a music store, he pulled displays to the ground behind him, slamming through the rear exit and sprinting out the back alley to hail a cab. Keeping low until they'd pulled into traffic, his pursuers never saw him. Once away from downtown, he instructed the cab driver to make two consecutive left turns and head back the way they'd come.

Even from a street away, Ethan could see that the safe house was burning to the ground. Paying off the driver, he ran the rest of the way.

"Sarah!" Ethan cried, stunned by the smoke billowing from the safe house as firefighters continued to battle the flames. Scanning the crowd as he pushed past the police officers, Ethan called again, "Sarah! No, please. Sarah!" This couldn't be happening.

Finally Ethan spotted her, wrapped in a blanket, her face smudged and dirty. Her hair was damp and sticking to her forehead. She was the most beautiful thing he'd ever seen.

Racing over, Ethan pulled her tightly to his chest, right next to his beating heart. "Sarah," he murmured in relief.

"Ethan," she replied, dropping her blanket to hold him back as tightly. "You came."

"I will always come for you," he said and then asked, "Teddy and Charlie?"

"They're fine," Sarah said.

"Ethan."

He looked up at his name, maintaining his hold on Sarah, unwilling to release her. When had the need to save her morphed from a duty to a need?

"Brigitte. What are you doing here?" Ethan said.

"I came to speak with Sarah," Brigitte said. "I was still here when the bomb exploded."

"Bomb?" Shocked, Ethan glanced at Sarah for confirmation. "A bomb?"

"Yes," Sarah said. "And there were gunmen out back. If Teddy hadn't gone back for his dinosaurs, we would have been shot."

Winding his fingers into her hair, he pulled her head to his chest, cradling her against him, not caring for the moment if she could hear the real fear in his heartbeat.

"Thank you, Brigitte," Ethan said. "For saving them."

"I didn't, Ethan. Sarah saved me…and the children. She was…incredible," Brigitte said and Ethan noticed that she too was smudged and wilted.

Sirens sounded and Ethan watched as two black Ford Explorers turned onto the end of the street. For the moment, their progress was halted by the emergency vehicles but Ethan knew that they were coming for him. And he knew equally well that they wouldn't protect Sarah and Teddy and Charlie. Someone was truly out to get him, to kill him, and anyone else associated with him.

"Sarah, get Teddy and Charlie and their things," Ethan said, pulling back. She nodded and moved away. "Brigitte, I need your help."

"Anything, Ethan," Brigitte said. "Sarah saved my life."

"Let me take your car…and cover for me. I have to protect them," he said, nodding in Sarah and the boys' direction.

"Here." Brigitte pushed her car keys into his hand. "Two-tone beige, 1986 Ford F-150 pickup, no GPS tracking or roadside assistance. Bequeathed by my grandfather. I'll say I leant it to a friend and then report it missing in a day or so. Go. Get them away from here."

Ethan pulled Teddy into his arms as he directed Sarah to the pickup, keeping a guiding hand in the small of her back. Belting the boys together into the middle seatbelt, Ethan pulled the pickup away from the curb, made a U-turn and drove away from the approaching Ford Explorers. And away from Washington, DC.

Sarah sang songs and told stories to the boys until they fell asleep, Teddy leaning against her and Charlie curled against Ethan's leg.

"Ethan?" Sarah touched him lightly on the arm, her voice quivering as she spoke.

"It'll be okay, Sarah," he said, trying to reassure her. But she began to weep quietly, burying her face in her arms. Pity and shame pulled at his heart. "I'm so sorry, Sarah."

Sniffing, she hiccupped a few times. "Don't be sorry, Ethan. I just wish…never mind." Chuckling wetly, she said, "I'm going to spend a fortune on therapists for these kids after all this."

Chuckling lightly, Ethan replied, "I'll help you pay."

She laughed a little more confidently. "I should think so."

Charlie shifted against his leg and she murmured comfort to him.

Cradling her cheek in his palm, he wiped her tears away with his thumb. "You are amazing, Sarah."

"I just needed a little cry," she said, shrugging. "Why is this happening?"

"I seem to be caught up in some sort of conspiracy and until I can figure out who's pulling the strings on this one, my life isn't worth a penny." He glanced aside at Sarah. "And, I'm afraid, by association, you're in danger, too."

"But that last attack came when you were out, when you were known to be out," Sarah said.

Ashamed to admit his error in judgment, Ethan continued looking forward as he said, "I...uh...told them about you. Not you specifically. They still have no record of who you are but that won't take them long. If only I had figured out what was going on sooner, I wouldn't have let them know and the house wouldn't have been incinerated and maybe you could have taken the first flight home. Now...well, I just don't know."

"What are we going to do?" she said, all the light extinguished from her eyes.

"We'll take Interstate 81 south to Knoxville, Tennessee and then we can take 40 across to Little Rock, Arkansas. My father lives outside there," Ethan said.

"Tennessee? Arkan—?" she said.

Ethan continued, nodding, "If we can get to Little Rock, we should be able to hide Brigitte's truck at my father's and get a vehicle from him. Then I think we should head for Colorado and drop off the grid."

"Uh," Sarah said and she looked as stunned as she sounded. "That's a long way."

"Yes," he said. "At nine o'clock tomorrow morning, when I fail to show for my hearing, I become a fugitive from justice. If they get to Owen or Bella and learn your identity...well, I'm not sure how far we'd have to go to keep you safe."

Sarah blanched. "But if you solve this *conspiracy*, you'll be free of it all?"

He shrugged. "That's my plan. I haven't figured out the logistics of it yet apart from getting you and the boys to a place of safety."

"What logistics need to be solved?" she inquired calmly.

"Money. Communications. Intelligence. They'll have a trace on all my bank accounts, my phones, my computers, everything," he said.

"I can get money," Sarah said.

"I don't want you to have to—" Ethan said.

"Actually, I think I can get all of those things," Sarah said as she pulled out her cell phone and dialed.

Ethan reached out and grabbed the phone, cutting off the call. "What are you doing?" he said tersely.

Holding out her hand, she demanded to know, "Do you trust me? Because it sounds to me like it's you and me together. Trust me, Ethan."

Struggling with himself, he finally conceded the battle. "I trust you," he said, his voice husky with emotion, handing back the cell phone.

"Hi Dad," she said when the call connected. "I know. We ran into some unexpected trouble but we're fine. Safe and sound. The National Gallery terrorist attack in Washington, DC. We're witnesses. Do you think you could let Johnny Parsons know? Tell him it would make a good story. Say that we were rescued by Ethan Lange…L-A-N-G-E…suspended FBI agent."

Ethan grabbed for the phone again but Sarah shifted out of reach. "Tell Johnny Parsons that I need a clean satellite phone and a clean laptop with connection. Did you get that, Dad? Please tell him exactly what I said. Tell him to meet me at Little Rock, Arkansas tomorrow at—" She turned to Ethan.

"Eleven o'clock in the morning," he said. *I cannot believe I'm letting her do this.*

"At eleven o'clock in the morning at the—" Sarah stopped, waiting for Ethan to fill in the blanks.

"The big tree by the parking lot in Allsopp Park," he said.

"The big tree in Allsopp Park," Sarah said. "Dad, can you transfer five thousand dollars into my chequing account? Please send three thousand of that with Johnny. Thanks,

Dad. I love you. They're asleep right now but I'll give them a big kiss from Grandpa. Thanks, Dad. Bye."

"Who is Johnny Parsons?" Ethan asked quietly when she'd ended the call.

"He's a close friend. He and David were roommates in University and they were both recruited into CSIS at the same time," she said. "Johnny left the Service after David died and became an investigative reporter for the New York Times, a real bull mastiff when it comes to a good story. He'll help us."

A reporter. Great, Ethan mused wryly. "Are you sure you can trust him?" he said.

"Yes, Ethan," she said. "I can trust him and he will not betray you either, even if only on my account."

They rode in silence for a time. Ethan thought that Sarah had fallen asleep with her head against the passenger side window until she spoke.

"Why are we meeting Johnny so close to your father's house? Won't it lead the bad guys right to his door?" she asked.

"My father can take care of himself," he replied.

She nodded and then turned back to the window. He almost didn't hear her soft voice, saying, "I'm scared, Ethan."

"I know," Ethan said. "But, I promise, I will protect you."

CHAPTER 11

They reached Little Rock at 9:30 am after sixteen hours of driving, interrupted by a six hour rest at a dingy, motel just west of Knoxville. Ethan took the 530 south and then turned onto Pine Road, following the familiar route to his childhood home.

By the time they reached the house, Ethan's father was approaching the vehicle and Ethan noted the handgun he'd concealed behind his leg. Groaning out of the pickup, Ethan greeted his father.

His father's grim mouth relaxed into a smile. "It's been a while," he said, drawing Ethan into a hug, finishing with a kiss on the cheek. Surprised, Ethan couldn't remember more than two occasions when his father had shown him any affection beyond a pat on the shoulder. "It's good to see you, son," his father said.

Ethan smiled, feeling slightly bewildered but happy by his father's greeting. "You too, Dad. You're looking well."

"You're looking rather battered," his father said. He turned to watch Sarah lift the boys down from the pickup truck.

"Dad, this is Sarah, Teddy and Charlie. Sarah, this is Robert Lange, my father," Ethan said.

Sarah shook Robert's hand, gracing him with a smile. Charlie clung to her shoulders and Teddy pressed against her leg.

"We're pleased to meet you," she said.

"Come in," Robert said. "I've just made coffee. And I'm sure I could find some cookies."

"Cookie," Charlie said, smiling from the safety of his mother's arms.

"You go ahead in, Sarah, while I talk to my father," Ethan said.

Sarah looked back and forth between Robert and Ethan and then nodded. At the front steps, Charlie wiggled down and ran back to Ethan.

"Eefan. No go?" Charlie asked.

"I'm not going anywhere, Charlie. Go in with your mommy. I'll be in soon," Ethan said, ruffling Charlie's hair. His father quirked an eyebrow at the interchange but said nothing until the front door clanged shut behind the little family.

"Who is she, son?" Robert asked. "The children?"

"They're not mine, Dad. I should be so lucky," Ethan finished, regretfully.

"Then who are they?" Robert asked.

"People I intend to protect," Ethan said.

"You'd risk your life for them?" Robert asked.

"I'd do anything for them, Dad," Ethan said and he realized that it was true. After only a few days, albeit extremely eventful days, he'd become attached to Sarah and her children. Little Charlie had cracked open a space in his heart and, for some reason, Ethan couldn't seem to close it down again. Sarah and Teddy had slipped through as well. "I need your help, Dad," he said.

Robert hesitated and Ethan stiffened, bitterness returning. "Never mind. Just feed us and we'll be on our way."

"Ethan, son," Robert began, halting Ethan with a hand on his shoulder. "I know that our, uh, relationship hasn't always been smooth. Your mother was the one who dealt out the love and affection and I was supposed to be wisdom and discipline." Robert sighed. "Son, I...I want you to know...I love you...and I'm proud of you, always have been. That night—it was never your fault. I'm, uh, sorry to have allowed you to carry the blame."

Robert pulled Ethan close, hugging him tightly, and Ethan could feel the wetness of tears against his neck. Stunned by his father's show of emotion, it took Ethan a moment to reciprocate the embrace. He felt his world shift just a little and then a whole lot more as he gripped his father tightly to him. The words sounded like a rehearsed speech but they were exactly the words that Ethan had craved to hear for so many years.

Pulling back and wiping his eyes on his sleeve, Robert brought them back to the task at hand. "Sorry, son. I've been waiting a long time to tell you that. Now, tell me what you need."

It took a moment for Ethan's roiling emotions to settle so he could respond. "If I could leave this pickup truck here and take old Jimmy? This vehicle belongs to a colleague and she'll need to report it stolen soon or she'll find *herself* in front of an enquiry panel. The old Jimmy has no GPS or any other way for them to track us. Do you still have the fake plates?"

"Of course," Robert said. "What undercover officer ever gives up his fake license plates?"

Ethan grinned. "I thought I'd head to Grandpa's cabin in Pitkin and disappear for a while. It would give me a base of operations from which to investigate."

"That's a good place to hide. But how will you investigate from there?" Robert said.

"Sarah's husband worked for CSIS before he died and she's got a contact, a Johnny Parsons, who she says can get us a satellite phone and a clean laptop," Ethan said.

"Johnny Parsons," Robert repeated thoughtfully. "Is he that government watchdog?"

"I'm not certain. She says he's an investigative reporter and she did call him some type of dog," Ethan said.

"Very good," Robert said decisively. "Let's get this truck out of sight. I'll call Stevie to come and we'll dump it northeast toward the Canadian border and then we'll wipe it clean, no traces. You and I can attach the plates to old Jimmy and fill it with gas and provisions. Can you stay for lunch?"

"We're meeting this Parsons fellow in Little Rock at eleven. We shouldn't take too long," Ethan said. He was struggling to keep up with the changes in his father. People really could change. "Look, Dad, I don't want to put you at risk."

"Ethan, no risk is too great for one of my sons." Robert clapped Ethan on the shoulder, the unexpected weight causing him to flinch. He pulled back, scanning Ethan's body. "Let me see."

"It's not necessary, Dad."

"Don't be difficult. Just lift your shirt and let me see." The entire left side of Ethan's chest was a purpling mass of bruises. "Do you want me to bind your ribs?"

"I don't think I could stand it. I just need to get us to Colorado and then I can recover," Ethan said.

"I've probably got some painkillers you can take with you," Robert said.

Together, they prepared the green 1984 GMC Jimmy, cleaning, filling, wiping and loading extra gas, a camp stove, pots, dishes, nonperishable foods, blankets, candles, matches, bear spray, solar powered security cameras, flares, a hunting rifle, ammunition and anything else that might be of use. Finally, at ten thirty, Ethan decided that they'd better head into Little Rock to meet with Johnny.

Preceding his father into the house, Ethan paused for a moment at the doorway to the lounge to enjoy the loving interaction between mother and sons, remembering another mother who loved her sons.

Eventually Sarah noticed the men watching her and looked up. "Hi. Is everything okay?"

"Yes," Ethan replied. "It's getting late, though. We need to meet Johnny."

"Mommy, I don't want to go. I like this show," Teddy whined from his position cross-legged before the old nineteen inch television.

"They can stay here, Sarah," Robert offered kindly.

"Oh, I...thank you but...they..." Sarah's protest ground to a halt.

"Mama, eat? Mama, hungwy," Charlie begged.

Ethan took Sarah's hand. "They'll be fine here. I promise," he said. "We really need to go."

Caution-borne reluctance gnawed at Sarah.

"Sarah," Robert said gently. "I have quite a bit of experience with boys. I might not have been the perfect substitute mother to them after their own mother died and perhaps a less than ideal father but I'm quite a popular grandfather."

Feeling her protective instincts relax a little, Sarah allowed a smile to grow slowly on her face, nodding once to accept his offer.

Robert bent over to boy height, clapping his hands enthusiastically, drawing the boys' attention. "Hey fellas, how would you like to see Ethan's best toys and then I'll make you his favorite meal...flapjacks and maple syrup."

"Yeah! Hurray!"

Sarah pulled the boys close and gave them their final instructions, reminding them to behave; reminding them to be careful...until Ethan finally took her hand and pulled her out the door in spite of her protests.

"Are you sure?" she said. "He wasn't the perfect father. Isn't that what you said? Are you sur—" Ethan pulled her close and stopped her protests with a kiss. Astonished into silence, she followed him to his father's vehicle, a blue 2007 GMC Jimmy. Robert Lange was a man of loyalty; loyalty to his sons, his country and his truck.

Pulling into the parking lot of Allsopp Park, Sarah spotted Johnny leaning against the 'very tall tree' with a large black bag slung over his shoulder. He was a thin man, willowy in appearance, taller than David, taller even than Ethan's six feet by a good three inches. His long black ponytail topped a deeply tanned face and intelligent pale blue eyes.

Ethan insisted on carefully surveying the area through the pair of binoculars he had borrowed from his father before he would allow Sarah to approach the reporter. And even then, he remained behind to keep watch.

Finally released to greet her friend, Sarah jogged over, waving and smiling. "Johnny!" she said and he lifted her into his arms enthusiastically, kissing her loudly on the cheek.

"Sarah, my girl! How have you been?" Johnny asked. "And what on earth are you doing in Little Rock, Arkansas? Allsopp Park? Big tree? Do you have any idea how difficult it was to find this spot? There are big trees everywhere around here!"

Sarah laughed, enjoying Johnny's familiar banter. *Good ole' Johnny.* "But I'm so glad you made it," she said. "You are a sight for sore eyes."

Sobering quickly, Johnny demanded to know, "What's going on Sarah?"

"It's a long story, Johnny, but one I would like to tell you." And Sarah proceeded to do just that, finding a nearby bench and resting there. Beginning with the terror attack at the National Gallery and Ethan's courage in rescuing them, she continued on through the murder of the witnesses and the subsequent attacks on Ethan and then on her and the boys.

"Do you think it would make a headline?" she said.

"Hmmm. Perhaps," Johnny said pensively. "But I want to meet him."

She chuckled. "Leave him be, Johnny. Did you get me what I asked for?"

"Indeed," Johnny said and then he handed over the bag he was carrying, opening it and showing her each item. "One clean satellite phone. One clean laptop with satellite connection. Three thousand dollars. Is he worth this, Sarah?"

"God put him in our path for a reason," Sarah said.

"And?" Johnny said, raising an eyebrow of concern.

"And I trust him," she said.

"Do you love him?" Johnny asked in that brazen openness he was known for.

"Johnny, I'm not looking for love, you know that," she said.

"I still want to meet him," he repeated firmly.

Sarah chuckled at the man's tenacity. "Then I shall introduce you. Come." She led him over to Robert's GMC Jimmy which to Sarah's surprise was empty. "Ethan?" she called. Searching around, Ethan materialized as if out of thin air. Startled, Sarah wondered aloud, "How did you do that?" When Ethan just shrugged, narrowing his eyes to study Johnny warily, she shrugged in resignation and introduced the men. "Johnny Parsons, this is Ethan Lange."

The men shook hands firmly, each clearly judging the other.

Johnny began his interrogation. "*The* Ethan Lange who is currently under investigation?"

"And if I am?" Ethan's voice was hard.

"You realize that Eleanor 'Bibi' Neweather-Baker, the widow of Senator Tom Baker, scheduled her bid for senate to coincide with the date of the enquiry of the rogue undercover officer responsible for her husband's death, even rescheduling it when the enquiry was postponed due to the terror attack on the National Gallery?" Johnny said.

Ethan looked shocked as he slowly shook his head.

"Did you realize that, although the name Ethan Lange has never been associated with the heroic rescue of Canadian widow, Sarah Maier, and her two young sons, his name has been leaked to the press as the rogue officer responsible for Tom Baker's death?" Johnny said.

"I suppose it shouldn't surprise me," Ethan said, resignation in his voice. "And I accept the responsibility for my actions, fair or foul. Will you help us Mr. Parsons?"

"I don't care what you say for yourself Mr. Night crawler, I only care what you intend for my Sarah." Johnny's face was hard as he studied Ethan closely.

Fearing that an animosity was growing between the two men, Sarah intruded, "Johnny, that's not—"

But Ethan waved away the arrogance of the statement. "It's all right, Sarah. I don't intend anything except to protect her and Teddy and Charlie. Will you help us?" Ethan insisted on an answer.

"Help the man who saved our Sarah?" Johnny's face broke into a broad grin. "Of course."

CHAPTER 12

Back at Ethan's boyhood home, Sarah immediately went in search of her children finding them with Robert, deeply involved in a game involving toys soldiers and rubber balls which seemed to require frequent growling and cheering accompanied by enthusiastic high-fives. Ambivalently accepting their desire to continue their game, Sarah went to the kitchen to see if there was lunch for her and Ethan. The dishes in the sink indicated that Robert and the boys had already eaten.

Turning at the sound of running water, Sarah glimpsed Ethan through the open door of the washroom adjacent to the kitchen. He was removing the bandages over his eyebrow and beneath his chin, leaning close to the mirror to examine his stitches. Her eyes moved from his chin up to his lengthening blonde hair, noting the curls which gave his rugged exterior a gentler appearance. He was a handsome man.

As Ethan carefully pulled his shirt over his head, Sarah took a step toward him. She knew she should warn him of her presence, or simply turn away, but she continued forward, drawn to him by...No. This could not be passion. It was simple attraction, the emotional connection of experiencing something terrible together.

As Ethan turned to examine his ribs in the mirror, Sarah glimpsed the mass of bruising on his side. Before she thought better of it, she was beside him, touching him, turning him by the shoulders so she could better see his injuries. Pity, and something else, filled her heart.

"Ethan, why didn't you tell me? That must be very painful." Tenderly, she traced the bruise, feeling the heat from the wound. "Baby, how could you let it get this bad?"

Raising her eyes, his gaze caught and held hers. His breathing deepened and his eyes grew darker, hotter. What had she said? What had she done to provoke that expression in his eyes? Not more than an hour ago, she'd denied any romantic feelings for Ethan but now...what was happening?

Dropping his head, he captured her lips. When she moved closer, he deepened the kiss, sweeping his hands up her back. Bewildered and uncertain, she stepped back from him, breaking the kiss.

"I...uh...I'll get some...lunch for us," she said, turning abruptly away.

"Look in the fridge," he said, his voice husky and deep. "I'll join you shortly. I just want to get rid of these stitches."

Sarah didn't want to think about what that kiss could mean. She wanted lunch, nothing more. Finding a couple of foil wrapped plates in the ancient refrigerator, Sarah uncovered the leftover chicken, mashed potatoes and carrots and placed them in the microwave.

As Sarah and Ethan ate silently in the kitchen, Teddy, Charlie and Robert joined them, the boys chatting excitedly about their adventurous afternoon capturing dragons, chasing pirates and *bonging* the bad guys. Before long, Ethan left the room to gather his belongings and Sarah and Robert were left alone in the kitchen. Rather than listen to the adults talk, the boys decided to investigate the new kittens under the front porch.

Robert gathered the dirty dishes into the sink and added soap and hot water.

"Robert?" Sarah began, remaining at the table where she was out of his line of vision "Can I ask you something personal?"

"Okay," Robert said, glancing back at her over his shoulder.

"When Ethan mentions his childhood...well, it isn't usually with much...warm feeling...and yet you seem quite lovely," Sarah said.

"Lovely? Just what every man wants to be called," Robert replied sardonically. "The man I was when Ethan and his brothers were young is not the man I am today. You see, someone wonderful came into my life a few years back."

"Someone?" she asked, feeling her brows furrow.

"God, actually," Robert said. "When my wife died, I was very angry…with God, with the church, with my children for needing her. My Rachel was such a fine woman of faith and I always relied on her to keep us on the right path. With her gone, I found myself floundering. The boys were young and Ethan especially missed the tender care of his mother.

"I brought my sister, Anne, to live with us for a time. Trying to pass off the responsibility for their nurturing, I suppose. It was a disaster. She and Ethan did not get along and I found myself having to discipline him really just for missing his mother. The night he came sobbing into my bedroom in the middle of the night calling for *Mommy*, I sent Anne home."

Robert sighed heavily. "I really did do my best." His shoulders slumped. "No, that's not true. There are many things I could have done better. It was after my eldest son, Ryan, had his first baby, a little girl…a tiny, new life…that I realized there was a hole in my heart and it was larger than even my own Rachel could have filled. I began to attend a local Wesleyan church and after a struggle and surrender, I let God into my life. I have managed to repair my relationship with Ryan and Stevie but Ethan was the son I had hurt the most and…I will admit that I've been dragging my heels on this one, fearing his rejection. God brought you here, Sarah, and I'm grateful."

"I certainly never expected to be caught up with an FBI agent and a terrorist but this is where I seem to be so I'll trust God for the rest," Sarah said.

"You'll watch over my son's heart, won't you?" Robert said.

"I'll watch over both our hearts," she replied. That promise was easy to make. She had no interest in being hurt again. Nor in hurting Ethan.

Robert seemed to accept her word and he moved away to say a few final words to Ethan as Sarah waited at the old Jimmy. Robert had prepared a backpack for each of the boys filled with treats, books and toys and was saying his last good-byes.

"I'll drive, Ethan," Sarah offered.

Ethan's eyes narrowed in suspicion. "Why?"

"You need to rest if your ribs are going to heal," Sarah said.

"I'm fine," he replied, pulling the keys from his pocket and moving toward the truck.

"Ethan. I will drive," she insisted.

He turned slowly to meet her gaze, his own eyes reflecting a sharpness clearly meant to express his displeasure with her insistence. "No."

Stepping over to him, she held out her hand. "I will drive and you will rest in the back." Ethan furrowed his brows but she continued anyway. "Could you please bring the boys after you say good-bye to your father?" she said.

A laugh burst forth from his lungs which he quickly supported with his arm across his ribs. "You're impossible...I am perfectly capable...never mind." Shaking his head, Ethan returned to the front porch.

"Bye, Dad," Ethan said.

"Good-bye, son. I love you," Robert said.

It took a moment for Ethan to respond but he did. "I love you, too."

Robert pulled a Bible from behind him to present to Ethan. "This was your mother's. I want you to have it."

With astonishment in his eyes, Ethan accepted the treasure. "Thanks."

Robert wrapped him in a fierce hug, lightening his grip and laughing apologetically when Ethan grunted at the pressure on his ribs.

"Teddy. Charlie. It's time to go," Ethan said when he seemed able to voice his words again.

"Say good-bye," Sarah called to the boys.

"Bye-bye, Papa Bert," Charlie said, wrapping his arms around Robert's legs. Robert bent and lifted him, hugging him tightly.

"Perhaps we'll meet again, Charlie-boy," Robert said.

Charlie nodded enthusiastically.

Teddy seemed to be studying the ground between his shoes as Charlie ran off to hug Ethan's leg and then climb into the front seat of the truck at his mother's instruction.

Robert sat down on the edge of the porch, drawing Teddy closer to him.

Tentatively, Teddy asked, "Are you really Ethan's daddy?"

"Yes," Robert said.

"He scared me. But now I'm not scared of him. He plays with me." Teddy looked up to meet Robert's gaze.

"What's the matter, son?" Robert asked, stroking his thumb across the little boy's knuckles.

"Ethan's not my daddy," he replied simply.

"No, that's true," Robert said.

"I gots two grandpa's already, Grandpa Maier and Grandpa Johnson," Teddy said.

"Yes," Robert said.

Teddy looked up sadly. "What do I call you?"

"How about Papa Bert just like your brother?" Robert said.

Teddy's smile illuminated his entire face. "Is that okay?"

"Absolutely," Robert said, smiling.

Teddy flung himself into the man's arms and hugged him tightly, finishing with a loud smirchy kiss on the cheek.

"Bye, Papa Bert," Teddy said, waving over his shoulder as he skipped over to Ethan, taking his hand and smiling brightly up at him. Ethan smiled as he held his mother's Bible in one hand and Sarah's son in the other.

CHAPTER 13

B rigitte Wright-Smith sat outside the office of Agent Ronald McCreary of the Federal Bureau of Investigation's Internal Affairs Division, the man assigned to investigate the disappearance of Ethan Lange. Brigitte cursed Ethan. What she'd done, she'd done for Sarah in return for saving her life. *Now, here I am, about to face the inquisition…for Ethan's sake.* Brigitte sighed. As much as her anger set her against Ethan, she knew that he was no traitor. Allowing Borz Vakh to escape had been a reasonable operational decision, particularly given the fact that the building was surrounded by FBI agents and police officers. No one could have known that the mercenary would then go on to murder the senator rather than escaping. Brigitte paused. *Of course! Why had no one considered that the senator might already have been dead?*

Her thoughts were interrupted by McCreary's assistant.

"Ms. Wright-Smith. You're next!" He pronounced it as an edict rather than an invitation.

"Sit," McCreary instructed, gesturing toward the hard-back chair in front of the oversized wooden desk. He launched his attack without pause. "It seems, Ms. Wright that your missing pickup truck has been located just south of Columbus, Ohio, indicating that your *thieves* were heading for Canada. Now why, Ms. Wright, would someone steal your truck and then abandon it in Ohio?"

"Mrs. Wright-Smith," Brigitte corrected him grimly. "How am I meant to know the answer to that question, sir?"

"Your friend, uh…" He checked his notes. "Toller Grint, corroborates your story that he borrowed the truck from you but no one from his apartment complex can recall ever seeing him drive that type of vehicle. How do you explain that?" McCreary said.

"I'm not certain that it's my responsibility to," she replied haughtily.

A slap resounded around the room as Agent McCreary revealed his disgust with Brigitte's answers against the table top in the meeting room.

"How long have you known Ethan Lange?" McCreary asked.

"Ten years," Brigitte replied, much more careful with her tone of voice this time.

"After your divorce, why did you continue to see him?" McCreary asked.

"We both work for the FBI. We couldn't avoid each other forever," Brigitte said.

"When did you become romantically involved again?" McCreary asked.

Brigitte blushed furiously. "We are not romantically involved."

"You say that, and yet your colleagues speak of a definite relationship between you, beyond what one would consider professional," McCreary said.

"I don't know who you were speaking to but Ethan and I are no longer together and have not been for many years. We do not have a romantic relationship," she said firmly.

"Who decided? You or him?" McCreary asked.

"What difference does that make?" she said.

"All the difference in the world if one is considering whether an officer has acted as an accessory to a crime," McCreary said. Leaning back against the wall and folding his arms across his chest, McCreary responded, threat in his very manner and tone, "Allowing a known terrorist to escape could be viewed as an act of terror in and of itself. What are your rights in that circumstance?"

Brigitte paled.

Sarah drove through the evening and into the night, grateful each moment for Robert's thoughtfulness and intuition in packing bags for the boys. They were simply entranced by each and every item they pulled from the depths of the backpacks. Sarah stopped for a brief supper, allowing Ethan to continue sleeping on the back seat of old Jimmy but purchasing an extra sandwich that he could eat later. However, he didn't wake.

Finally at ten o'clock, Sarah felt herself drifting as she drove and began to scan for a motel. When another half hour passed, she gave up, turning into a small laneway which led only to the fence of a farmer's field. Laying a pillow beneath him like a mattress, Sarah curled Teddy up on the floor of the vehicle beside Ethan in the back of the truck, wrapping a blanket around him. She did the same for Charlie in the front. Checking that Ethan was okay, she tucked his blanket more firmly around him and then made a bed for herself on the front seat, locking them in and then falling asleep herself.

She woke to a gentle kiss on her cheek, looking up into the deep blue eyes of what? Passion? Desire? No. Tenderness certainly, blue-eyed tenderness.

"Morning," Ethan said, smiling at her, a smile that reached his eyes.

"Mmmm. Not the most comfortable bed I've ever slept in but not the worst either," she said. "Teddy and Charlie?"

"Sitting on the roof counting cows," Ethan said.

She smiled, thanking him for looking after them. "How are you feeling?" she asked.

"Still sore and pretty tired, to be honest, but much better," he said. "Thank you for the rest."

"My pleasure," she said. "Do you want me to drive again today?"

"Maybe later," he said but she could tell that he really meant *no-way, ho-say.*

"Sure," she said, chuckling lightly. "I need to find a toilet."

He chuckled. "There's a great big tree just over there." He pointed and she decided that trees were a lovely creation for so many reasons.

Ethan drove, taking the back roads whenever possible to avoid surveillance. They watched for mini-adventures along the way, allowing the boys to run and jump and basically expend their energy until they were ready for the wonders of Papa Bert's backpacks again.

As they crossed into Oklahoma, Ethan's attention shifted in intensity.

"What is it?" Sarah insisted on knowing.

"There's a helicopter," Ethan said. "It's been circling for the past half hour."

"How can you tell it's the same one you keep seeing?" she asked.

"The registration numbers," he said.

"Could it be a news helicopter or something like that?" she said.

"Possibly," he said, clearly unconvinced of that explanation. "I think we should alter our course. Grab the map and find us a side road."

Spreading the State of Oklahoma across her lap, she quickly scanned the grid to find their current location and hurriedly found a new way across. Turning right, Ethan took a small highway north, increasing speed to test whether the helicopter was actually interested in them.

"Ethan, look!" Sarah exclaimed as she pointed to the sign advertising helicopter tours. Ethan released his tension on a laugh, finding the next left turn to work their way back to the highway.

"Paranoia," he mumbled, shaking his head.

Finally, after days and days of traveling, they entered the tiny town of Pitkin, Colorado and passed right through it almost before they realized, taking the dirt road and then the long, long driveway to Ethan's grandfather's cabin. It was an A-frame log house with two bedrooms on opposite ends of a large multi-purpose lounge/kitchen/dining room, a large washroom complete with cast iron tub, and a small loft. Completely isolated, the cabin had been built on a slope in a meadow which was surrounded on three sides by tall evergreens. There was a deck off the front bedroom and a patio door off the side of the lounge. Directly out from the front bedroom, Sarah could see the meadow grass roughen to stony ground and, beyond that, a sparkling blue lake and then, the towering peaks of the Rocky Mountains.

"It's beautiful!" she exclaimed, awestruck by the splendor of the location.

Pulling out some of their provisions, she and Ethan made a simple supper and then they took the boys for a walk to the lake, stopping to skip stones and climb a few boulders. Expending the boys' energy temporarily, they returned so Sarah could put the boys to bed in the loft.

Teddy reached up from the covers to hug her. "Is this our home now?"

"For a little while," Sarah replied, smiling down at him.

"Does that mean Ethan's my daddy now?" Teddy asked.

Shocked by the question, Sarah stumbled through an answer. "Well…no…Ethan can't be your daddy unless…he would need to marry me. I would need to marry him."

"Oh. Okay," Teddy replied, content with her response, rolling onto his side and closing his eyes.

Sarah was shaken by the question. Did Teddy want a father? How could she have let someone into their life, not noticing how serious things had become? The intensity of that kiss at Robert's house, what did that mean? Passion? Friendship? Love? *I'm not looking for love.*

Prowling the lounge, Sarah dusted, rearranged, did *anything* to keep her mind and hands occupied as her mind bleated a shrill warning.

Ethan's unexpected touch on her shoulder made her jump and he stepped back, muttering, "Sorry."

"It's okay," she mumbled, pressing her hand to her chest to calm her rapidly beating heart.

"What's wrong?" he asked suspiciously.

"Nothing."

"Sarah." Her name was a reprimand.

"What do you believe about God?" she asked all in a rush, turning to face him. This was it, her way to settle this matter once and for all. His answer would tell her what she needed to know to squash these ridiculously romantic and terrifying thoughts about him.

Furrowing his brow at her, he responded warily. "I remember going to church before my mother died." His features softened for a moment. "She lined us up, slicking down our hair and telling us not to eat bugs in Sunday School, just to put them in our pockets for later."

Completely breaking her out of her introspection, Sarah released an astonished snort. "What? Which of you ate a bug in the first place making her feel she had to give you those instructions?"

Ethan shrugged, grinning. "Probably Stevie." He sobered. "After mom died, my father was angry most of the time. We stopped attending our church. I remember the minister coming out to visit us once and my father hollering at him and slamming the door in his face. When my Aunt Anne came to live with us, she dragged us boys to a different church, one with uncomfortable pews and lots of rules. After she returned to her own home, church ended. My father would take us hunting or hiking on Sunday mornings."

"What did you think of your Aunt?" Sarah asked, remembering what Robert had told her.

"Couldn't stand her," Ethan said. "She was mean and bossy and I guess she hated me too because she left before the school year ended."

"Your father told me that he asked her to leave because she was making you unhappy," Sarah said, unwilling to let Ethan carry another burden of blame that wasn't his to keep.

Surprised, Ethan said, "Really? I didn't know that."

"That's church," she said. "But what do you believe about God?"

"Oh, I guess I know that God is real and He's out there somewhere but, frankly, I guess he likes me about as much as Auntie Anne," Ethan said.

Surprised, Sarah asked, "What makes you say that?"

Ethan paused before answering and Sarah could see the wheels of confusion turning behind his eyes. "Sarah, I understand that you are a woman of faith. My mother was, too. I remember sitting on her lap while she read me Bible stories. I remember praying with her and I remember praying for her. While she was dying beside me in the car, I prayed harder than ever before. But, Sarah—" He leaned forward resting his elbows on his knees, studying the stain on the rug between his feet. "My mother died. And when she died, I guess God just walked right out on me. My mother's death changed everything about my life."

"Oh, Ethan." Sarah's heart ached for him. "Don't you think I felt that way when David died? I'd prayed and prayed for children and right when I was given the desire of my heart, my husband was taken from me."

Ethan nodded tersely, looking up to her face. "So you understand what I'm saying."

"No. No, I don't," she said. "God didn't promise that our lives would be free of pain, only that there was a higher purpose. He didn't promise to anaesthetize us from the realities of the world, only to love us enough to send his one and only son to die and rise again. In exchange for that sacrifice, all He asks is that we believe Him."

"But for what purpose, Sarah?" Ethan said.

"What do you mean?" she said.

"God didn't save my mother and I can't point to one single thing he's done in my life since." Ethan rose abruptly and strode away.

Compassion and the beginnings of comprehension spurred her retort. "He brought Teddy and Charlie into your life." Sarah stood and moved to her bedroom, halted by his next word.

"And?" he asked, looking directly ahead at his bedroom door. She turned to him, seeing only his back, his shoulders tense. "Do I have Teddy and Charlie?"

"They love you, Ethan. Why do you think Teddy was so confused about what to call your dad? He wants to be loyal to you but knows you aren't his father." Sarah remembered the little boy's question just that evening, the question that had so confused her.

"And?" he asked again.

"And what?" she asked, not having any idea how to answer him. *I'm not looking for love.*

Turning to her, he held her gaze across the space. "Sarah," he said. His voice held a warning and not a hint of humor.

"I care. Of course I care about you, Ethan." She watched his eyes brighten. "How could I not care about the man who saved my children?" She watched his eyes fall.

Dropping her gaze, she strode quickly up the stairs to the loft ostensibly to check on her sleeping children, trying to ignore the guilt she felt at the incomplete answer she'd given Ethan. Because she was very afraid that no matter how she felt about it, much more was happening between her and Ethan than she had ever imagined possible.

CHAPTER 14

Since Sarah's *declaration of disinterest* as Ethan thought of it, he'd thrown himself into solving the mystery of Bibi Baker and Borz Vakh using the equipment Johnny had procured for them. When he wasn't bent over the laptop, Ethan started spending more time on his own exploring and fishing, getting to know again his childhood retreat. Anything that took him away from the pang of sorrow he felt whenever he saw Sarah and knew that she saw him only as the guy who'd saved her kids, nothing more.

His grandfather's cabin, the house where his mother had been raised by her God-fearing parents, had been his absolute favorite place to be. Always seeming to understand Ethan's damaged heart and desire to match his brothers, his grandfather had spent hours exploring with Ethan when he was a boy. But once Ethan cut himself off from his family, he'd also cut his ties here. His grandfather had died five years ago, leaving this cabin to Ethan but Ethan had refused to change the name on the deed and claim it as his own, a fact that he hoped now might save their lives.

Ethan filled his canteen with water and pulled the rifle down from the rack over the fireplace slipping it over his shoulder and pulling his grandfather's ball cap on. *I've got to solve this puzzle, uncover this conspiracy and get Sarah and the boys safely home. Things between me and Sarah have become so uncomfortable. I thought that things were...possible. I don't understand what happened to change the easy relationship we'd had.*

"Eefan? Go outside?" Charlie hopped into the room, crawled up onto the back of the wooden sofa and along the back to the fireplace mantel, hanging there by his fingertips.

Ethan smiled fondly at the little boy who'd opened his heart. "I'm just going hiking, Charlie. I'll be back soon."

"Me go?" Charlie asked with his eyes full of hope.

Ethan shook his head. "I don't think Mama would let you come, honey." Sighing morosely, Ethan watched Charlie's eyes fall to the floor.

"Mama!" The little boy's voice rang through the cabin.

Sarah hurried into the room. "Yes, Charlie. Goodness sakes, I thought the ceiling had fallen in by the way he was yelling," Sarah said. Ethan noticed that her smiles never reached her eyes anymore and he supposed it was probably his fault.

"Me go Eefan?" Charlie climbed down and began to hop in front of his mother. "Pease, Mama, pease. Pease!"

She looked at Charlie but she didn't look at him and Ethan felt a sadness descend on his chest. He realized that it had been a week at least since she'd last spoken directly to him or met his gaze. *Why do I always make such a hash of relationships?*

"I'm sure Ethan wants some time alone, Charlie. We don't want to be a burden to him," Sarah replied.

"None of you are ever a burden to me, Sarah," Ethan assured her sincerely. "You are all welcome to come."

"Mama, pease! Hike Eefan?" Charlie begged, pulling himself up his mother's legs as though she'd agree if only he was taller.

Conceding, she took Charlie's little hand. "Okay, sweetheart, if Ethan doesn't mind. I'll get a granola bar for you. Do you have some water for him?" Sarah asked Ethan, not waiting for a response as she moved away to the cupboard to retrieve a snack bar for the little boy and then tuck it into his little pocket. "Be good and do what Ethan says."

Charlie nodded vigorously in agreement. Ethan held out his hand for the little boy and they set off together up the mountain. Ethan surprised himself with how much he enjoyed spending time with Sarah's children. He had never really spent much time with children. He and his brothers were close in age and had been raised as a brood rather than having any sort of mentoring relationship with each other.

Because of his father's disapproval of his time at the University of Colorado, application to the FBI and then, later, his recruitment into the CAUDO Project, Ethan had moved away from home after high school, not returning. So he had missed the births of his nieces and really had almost no relationship with them other than cards at birthdays and gift certificates for Christmas.

"Eefan wook!" Charlie called to him, crouching down and pointing out a particularly interesting pile of rocks.

"Stay back, Charlie." Ethan crouched beside the little boy. "Sometimes snakes like to hide in rocks like that." Ethan hoisted Charlie onto his shoulders where he could keep him out of harm's way and they carried on hiking up the side of the mountain, stopping for a snack overlooking a gorgeous mountain valley and then starting back down to the cabin.

"Nake?" Charlie asked from his perch on Ethan's shoulder.

"Yeah, buddy, those are the rocks we saw before," Ethan said. "Sometimes snakes like to hide in rocks."

"Nake," Charlie repeated, knocking Ethan's ball cap off as he pointed. Ethan reached down to pick up his hat.

The rattlesnake darted forward, plunging it's fangs into Ethan's arm just above the wrist. Jumping back, Ethan clutched Charlie close to avoid dropping him. The rattle-less snake fled.

"Nake. Ouch Eefan?" Charlie asked, concerned.

Dazed, Ethan realized that Charlie had tried to warn him of the snake but he'd not noticed it, too absorbed in his own thoughts. Ethan knew enough of rattlesnakes to know that even though they were well-known for their warning rattle, it wasn't a failsafe.

This was bad. Snake bite meant anti-venin. Anti-venin meant hospital. Hospital meant personal identification. He couldn't allow that. They'd only just come to a place of safety. He couldn't put Sarah and the boys at risk again. He would just treat the wound and hope for the best.

Ethan shifted Charlie to ride piggyback, wincing when the boy's knee bumped his still tender ribs. Back to the cabin they hiked. Charlie chattered about all they'd seen, the snake, the chipmunks and squirrels, the mountain lion and moose scat which he called poo-poo, something that would normally have amused Ethan; normally, when he hadn't just been bitten by a rattlesnake. And what about Charlie? How close had the little boy come to falling victim to the same snake? Ethan's heart clenched at the thought of Charlie hurt.

Ethan stopped frequently for sips of water. He was beginning to feel unwell but the swelling around the snakebite wound was minimal. Nearing the meadow and dropping Charlie to walk beside him, they finally arrived at the cabin.

"Charlie, you're back!" Teddy said, running over to greet his brother. "Come see what me and Mommy did. Ethan, Mommy and me built a fort from the logs and rocks and a big box from the shed." Charlie ran over to Teddy.

"I'll come over later, okay, Teddy. I'm not feeling well," Ethan replied.

Teddy's gaze fell. "Promise?" he asked beseechingly.

"I promise," Ethan assured him.

Teddy's gaze immediately brightened and he skipped off with his brother. Soon Ethan heard Sarah greeting the boys and asking Charlie about his hike. For once, Ethan was glad that Sarah was uninterested.

He went straight to the washroom, taking the first aid kit out of the cabinet, washing the wound. It was tender to the touch. He rubbed aloe vera over the wound optimistically and swallowed a few Pai Yao pills, a common Chinese remedy for snake bite.

He was starting to feel dizzy now. Taking a long drink of water, he put on the kettle to make some tea. Reclining on the sofa, he lowered his injured arm to the floor, keeping the wound below his heart using gravity to slow the spread of the venom. He didn't want to fall asleep but he thought the worsening nausea would probably discount that possibility. He wished he'd brought a bucket with him to the sofa.

"Ethan, are you better yet?" Teddy asked as he and Charlie and Sarah trooped inside.

"What do you mean, Teddy?" Sarah asked, removing Charlie's muddy shoes at the door, her back to Ethan.

"Ethan said he was sick before," Teddy said.

"Really?" Sarah asked, calling back over her shoulder. "Ethan, are you sick?"

"Nake," Charlie said.

"That's nice, sweetheart. All right, you monsters, go wash up and I'll start supper soon." Sarah stood, stretching out her back as the boys ran off to comply. "Ethan?" Finally noticing him, she moved quickly to his side, sitting on the coffee table beside him. "You're quite pale." She laid the cool palm of her hand against his forehead. "You are ill."

"I'll be fine," he replied but he could see the doubt in her eyes. His eyes lost focus at the exquisite sensation of Sarah running her fingers through his hair. Shifting closer, her leg knocked against his injured arm and he flinched, biting his lip to prevent himself from crying out. But a whimper must have escaped because she looked down, gently lifting his arm to examine it.

"Ethan," she exclaimed, her voice full of concern and compassion as she noticed the two puncture marks. "Snake. That's what Charlie meant! You were bitten by a snake?" Her eyes studied him closely and he saw the fear that glinted in the edges.

"I wish you'd teach him to speak more clearly then I would have known he was warning me," Ethan joked but the smile never reached his lips.

"We have to take you to the hospital immediately. Ethan, why didn't you tell me?" Her eyes filled with tears.

"Sarah, we can't go to the hospital. We'd need identification to get medical assistance. It would put us in the system again and they could track us. They could find Teddy and Charlie, Sarah." Ethan dropped his voice. "They could find you." He reached over with his uninjured arm to squeeze her fingers reassuringly. "I'll be okay. I've been bitten before. I'm not allergic." Shaking her head, she started to argue but he rested his fingers against her lips. "I'll be fine. Could I have some tea?" he asked, hoping to distract her from his wound by giving her a task to complete.

"Yes," she said. "Yes, I'll make you some tea." Gently, she lowered his arm to his side and moved away to make tea. Soon the boys came clambering back into the lounge but Sarah sent them up to the loft to play. She returned with the tea and some chicken broth, sitting on the coffee table again and presenting a teaspoonful of soup to him.

He chuckled lightly. "I can sit up and feed myself." But as he moved to rise, the room spun around and Sarah grabbed for him as he slipped back onto the sofa.

"I don't care who finds us, Ethan, we're going to the hospital," she said. "You're worth the risk."

He shook his head. "No, Sarah. Please. If you'll just help me, I'll be fine."

"No. Ethan. I can't. I care about you too much to see you hurt or ill." She shook her head vigorously, whispering, "I don't want to lose you."

Reaching out, he brushed his fingertips along her cheek, a weight lifting from his chest, a weight he hadn't realized he'd been carrying. "Truly?"

"Truly. Please let me help you," she said. "If we wait too long I don't know how I'll get you to the car. If I have to carry you, I'll be in traction for a month!"

He released a small smile. "I'll take care of you." He watched her eyes, lost in the warm depths of them, willing her to understand his devotion to her, beyond what she meant to him as a friend and the mother of Teddy and Charlie. "Sarah, what happened…between us? Tell me what I did wrong," he said pleading with her to give him the opportunity to rectify his actions or words.

Shaking her head, she assured him, "Nothing. You did nothing wrong."

"Something happened, Sarah. We were—" He paused. "Closer. Friends. More. Then suddenly you wouldn't talk to me or even look at me. What did I do wrong?"

"Nothing. Really," she said. He glared at her. At least he thought he was glaring. Sighing morosely, she capitulated, "The first night we arrived here, Teddy asked me if you were going to be his daddy now."

"Oh, Sarah. Why was that a problem? He's just a little boy. How is he to know that I don't have the makings of a good father?" Ethan said.

"Ethan, I'm not—" she said.

The weight hovered over him again. "Looking for love. I know, you've told me," he completed her thoughts tonelessly.

"Do you want to know why?" she asked, her voice soft, her expression haunted.

Furrowing his brow, he insisted, "I want to know why you've shut me out."

"I thought, when David died, that I had made a choice. That in praying for a child, for children, I had made a choice to put children ahead of David. I thought that this was the justice afforded me for putting my needs ahead of my husband's. Then I realized that that isn't the way God works. He doesn't bargain with us. He doesn't say, 'Well, if you want this then I'll take that away'. He loves us and wants to give us the desires of our heart. I don't know why David died. I don't know why your mother died but I am confident that it wasn't a punishment or a balancing of karma. I know who I believe in and I am convinced that He loves me too. I realized that I didn't have to feel guilty about David's death and that God wasn't upset with me for grieving, and that, in fact, He grieved with me."

"I wish I had your faith, Sarah."

"It's available for everyone, Ethan."

"Is that why you pulled away from me? Because I have no faith?" he asked.

"You have faith, Ethan. You just don't know it yet. And no, that's not why I..." She sighed. "Pulled away. After David died and I realized that God still loved me, I slowly adjusted to all that it meant to be a single parent. I understood that God would be the father my children needed. When—" She turned her mournful expression to him and stopped speaking.

"Sarah, just tell me," he said. "It can't possibly be any worse than what I'm thinking."

"I'm afraid of letting anyone into our lives that might change things for the children. I would rather spend the next eighteen years alone than do anything to harm them," she said.

"I would never hurt your kids," he assured her.

"But would you really become their father? I can't divert the plan for their lives just because I think I've fallen in—" She stopped. "How do I separate out what's best for them and what I want?"

The blue of his eyes deepened as he asked softly, "Sarah, do you...could you ever..."

"Oh, Ethan. Don't make me." Pulling back, she went to rise but he reached for her wrist, pulling her back to sit beside him.

"Sarah," he said, pleading with her for something he wanted badly.

Resolute, she refused him. "You can *Sarah* me all you want but I can't tell you what I don't understand myself."

As the reality of what she was saying filtered through his foggy brain, the pressure on his chest lightened and he hoped. "If I could become—how can I become—" He stopped. "What is the desire of your heart?"

"I thought I knew, but now I'm thinking there may be something more," she said enigmatically.

He still didn't get the answers he wanted but now he knew that he hadn't done anything wrong. His mind was too foggy to go beyond that thought. Except to think about her passion…compassion, he corrected himself. He didn't want to lose her. He just wanted…"Kiss me?"

Leaning in, she kissed him lightly on the cheek and then she didn't seem to be able to stop. She kissed him on the forehead and then the mouth, lingering there. Pulling back minutely, her breath tickled his lips as she spoke. "If we can't take you to the hospital, what can we do?"

"Our best," he replied, leaning in to kiss her once more.

She nodded at his words and went to prepare some supper for Teddy and Charlie, making sandwiches for her and the boys. She then let them watch television so she could stay by Ethan's side, retrieving a bucket and a cool cloth at his request. When he began to throw up, she refused to listen to his excuses any longer.

"That's it. Enough!" Her words were fierce enough to attract the boys' attention. "I'm calling Johnny. You're getting worse." Sarah stood abruptly, moving away to the satellite phone. Ethan heard the mumble of conversation but he was starting to have difficulty following the meaning of the words. His arm was throbbing and the swelling had spread.

"A vet," Sarah said and Ethan thought maybe he was worse off than he'd thought because he had no idea what she was talking about. "Johnny says we should take you to a vet. We can just say that we have no healthcare coverage or something. I don't know. I don't want to lie. Maybe we can pay for the serum and administer it ourselves. I don't know, but Johnny says that vets around here will have anti-venom on hand. Do you know where there is a vet around here?" she asked.

There was a delay as the words sank in but eventually Ethan was able to respond. "Yes. Gunnison's off Highway 50. I can give you directions. Can you drive? I don't think I'd better."

"Teddy, Charlie. Quick and go pee, we need to go see someone about Ethan's snakebite."

"Okay Mama."

"Okey-dokey Mommy."

The boys ran off and soon returned. Sarah helped Ethan sit up straight and then stand. He leaned heavily on her as she led him to old Jimmy, belting him in and then belting the boys into their seats in the back. She ran back into the cabin, returning with a couple of toys and two water bottles, handing the former to the back seat and the latter to Ethan.

"Go straight out the laneway and then turn right onto 50," Ethan said. His voice was husky and his eyes were drooping. He took a sip of water to try and fix…something. *What?*

Sarah nodded and followed his instructions, resting her hand on his leg as she drove.

"Ethan? Baby?" He snapped to awareness at her words. "You need to stay with me, sweetheart. We're coming into Gunnison. Where do I go?"

"Um. Turn left on North—no South twelfth. Left on South twelfth" he said.

"The number or the word?" she asked and he squeezed his eyes shut to try and picture the sign.

"The number," he said finally.

She nodded and her hand left his leg as she turned the truck. He missed the connection immediately.

By the time they reached the veterinary clinic, most of the lights were out along the road.

"Ethan, the clinic's closed."

Her hand was back on his leg again and he found it much easier to think about that than the words she was speaking. He forced himself to concentrate. *Vet. Closed.* "Vet," he said. His tongue kept getting in the way of his words. "The vet lives next door."

Slipping out the driver-side door, Sarah rounded the front of the truck and opened Ethan's door. "Ethan." Lightly, she slapped his cheeks. "Ethan." He knew his eyes were open because he could plainly see the anxiety on her face. *What's she so worried about? Me? Really? Me?* "Ethan, when this is over I am going to beat you senseless for scaring me like this and then I'm going to kiss you senseless so you never think you're not worth the risk again. Do you understand?"

Grinning stupidly, he nodded at her. *Maybe she could love me!*

Turning away, she stopped and turned back to kiss him hard on the mouth. "Don't you dare die on me," she commanded. "Teddy, climb up front please and keep Ethan awake. I'll be right back."

Soon, the two boys were sitting on his lap talking to him and patting his cheeks, ordering him to stay awake. Sarah had left the car door open so he could hear her voice as she pleaded with someone to help.

"He's been bitten by a snake, a rattlesnake, I think. Please help us. You must have some anti-venom," Sarah pleaded.

Soon a stranger appeared and helped Ethan down from the truck and into a dimly lit building that smelled of antiseptic and flea spray.

"Sir? Sir." The voice demanded his attention. "Do you know what type of snake you were bitten by?"

"Western Rattler," Ethan said. His voice felt thick. Was that possible, for a voice to be thick?

"You're certain?" the man asked as he checked Ethan's pupils and his pulse.

What? Nake? Sssnake? "Yes," Ethan replied definitely.

"Are you allergic to anti-venin?" the man asked.

"No," Ethan replied.

The vet reclined him on a clean metal table, allowing his injured arm to lie below the edge of the table. He returned in a few minutes with an intravenous hook-up, a bag of clear liquid, a vial and a syringe. Carefully, he cleaned Ethan's wound and then hooked up the IV.

"Ma'am?" the vet said. What was his name? "I can take the little boys to see the puppies if you like?"

"Yes. No. Yes, thank you," Sarah said.

~ 111 ~

Ethan could hear the barking puppies and Charlie's squeals of delight. Soon his view of the kennel door was blocked by Sarah as she bent over him, kissing lightly on the mouth. His responses were so sluggish that he wasn't able to return the kiss before she stepped away.

"Please be okay," she beseeched him. And then she kissed him again and this time he was prepared, returning her kiss, reaching up to wind the fingers of his uninjured hand into her hair, holding her against him until he needed to breathe.

Ethan sighed, already beginning to feel significantly better. Enjoying the feel of Sarah's hand on his leg and the care in her voice, Ethan closed his eyes, relaxing into the coolness of the metal table.

Dozing on and off, Ethan opened his eyes to see the vet beside him taking his pulse. He slept again, awakened a while later by Charlie's chatter describing the puppies he'd seen. From where he sat on the table beside Ethan's head, the little boy reached down from time to time to pat Ethan's cheek. Ethan leaned into his side, enjoying the little boy smell of him, all fresh air and dirt. The next time he roused, Ethan thought he was alone. Feeling so much better but still tired, he pushed up onto his elbows to survey the room.

"How are you feeling?" Surprised, Ethan turned to see the vet beside him. He was older, maybe sixty or so. He had a kind, round face bordered by a ring of fine, white hair.

"Much better, thank you. Where's Sarah?" Ethan said.

"I showed her a place where she could put the boys down to sleep. She'll be right back I assure you. She hasn't left your side for more than five minutes the entire time. You're a lucky man. A devoted wife. Two adorable sons."

Ethan smiled in spite of himself. "Thank you for your help."

The man responded seriously. "Do me a favor? Don't ever tell anybody."

"You have my word," Ethan assured him, shaking his hand. "Uh, who are you?"

"Best if you don't know," the vet replied, smiling grimly.

Once the man was satisfied that Ethan had received enough anti-venin, he released them, refusing any kind of payment. Guiding them back to the cabin, Ethan went straight to bed as ordered, listening as Sarah put the boys to bed. He expected to fall asleep quickly as his body recovered but he couldn't sleep. So he went out to make some hot cocoa, surprised to find Sarah sitting on a stool, bent over the counter. He thought maybe she'd fallen asleep until he heard her quiet sobs.

"Sarah," he called softly to her, watching her startle and straighten, brushing her hands across her face.

"Hi. Couldn't sleep," she said abruptly, keeping her face turned away from him and her voice falsely light. But he wasn't so easily fooled.

Resting the palm of his hand on her back, he said, "Everything's okay. I'm fine. There's no need to be sad"

"Sad?" Her shoulders shuddered again. "I am so angry with you."

Surprised by the angst in her voice, he asked, "Angry?"

She spun to face him. "You weren't careful, Ethan! You could have died."

"But I didn't die. I'm fine." Firmly, he took her by the shoulders. "Why are you angry with me?"

Instead of answering, she flung her arms around his neck. "I don't want to lose you!" She began to cry again and he held her tightly, reveling in the feeling that she cared for him, perhaps even loved him, or maybe could someday. His enjoyment, however, was interrupted when she slapped him on the chest.

"Ouch!" he complained, shocked by her behavior.

"Don't ever do that again! You are too important to three people I know very well. Don't ever treat your life so lightly again! Please!" she said.

Feeling a deep desire to smile, he suppressed it, afraid it might land him another smack. "All right," he agreed, stepping back and raising his hands in surrender. "I promise. You don't need to hit me again."

She laughed, releasing the tension. "Sorry for smacking you."

Drawing her close again, he kissed her on the forehead. "It didn't really hurt, just surprised me."

She rested her face in the crook of his neck, her deep exhalation tickling him.

"I don't want to lose you," she repeated.

"I don't want to be lost, not from you," he said and he held her close for a long time. "Um, Sarah?" She nodded in response to the question in his voice. "You've beaten me now," he said. "Wasn't there something else you promised to do?"

Confused, she pulled back and then slowly grinned, a blush flooding her cheeks. "I believe there was," she replied, proceeding to kiss him senseless and then send him off to his bed so she could return to her own, his heart light and grateful for...the Western Rattler of all things.

CHAPTER 15

C oming up beside Ethan where he sat hunched over the laptop at the kitchen counter, Sarah smiled at his concentration. He was making progress in his investigation of Bibi and Tom Baker as well as the history of Borz Vakh, exchanging information with Johnny on public access chat rooms and blogs, using code words and secret signals, all very clandestine. In the evenings, he reviewed what he'd discovered with Sarah. The trust that implied warmed her heart, especially when he told her that talking it through with her helped him process the information more fully.

"Hi," she said when her presence didn't call his attention.

Reaching for her hand, he pulled her closer, saying, "What's up, Beautiful?"

Immediately, she checked the bandage on his wrist. He smiled at her. He always seemed so pleased when she took care of him. What a difference a snake bite had made in her life. The fear of losing Ethan had crumbled the walls of her resistance. Risking her emotions was worth it when the alternative was losing Ethan. God had an interesting way of doing things.

She smiled to herself. "Teddy wants to go exploring but Charlie's still napping. I wondered if you could—"

"I'll stay with him," Ethan said. "You two go on. Take the rifle and the bear spray."

"I don't know how to shoot, Mr. Action Man," Sarah said.

"Hmmm. I need to remedy that. Take the bear spray and make lots of noise. Tell me which direction you're heading," Ethan said.

"Being a little bossy, aren't we?" Sarah teasing him.

"Sarah, I'm not trying to be *bossy*, but this is the true wilderness, full of bears and wolves…and snakes, if you recall. I want you to be safe," he said.

Concerned, Sarah asked, "Should we wait for you?"

"If you take the bear spray and stay away from the lake, you should be fine," Ethan said.

"Thanks, now I only feel a little intimidated." She leaned in to kiss his cheek but he tilted his head at the last second and met her lips with his own, smiling against her mouth. He couldn't seem to stop kissing her lately, she mused.

Sarah and Teddy set out to tromp the meadow in the opposite direction to the lake, finding a slump of ground which they decided looked exactly like a dragon's nest, weaving a story of the creature and its adventures. Following that, they spent some time racing to the top of the hilly ground and then rolling down into the nest again. After two trips down the hill, though, Sarah chose to watch and cheer as Teddy continued again and again. *I'm too old to roll down hills any longer!*

Returning an hour or so later, Sarah and Teddy bellowed out the words to *I've Got a Mansion, Just Over the Hilltop…* but their singing was interrupted by Ethan's desperate shout of, "Charlie!" When the call resounded, Sarah took Teddy by the hand and ran the rest of the way to the cabin, finding Ethan emerging from the building with a flashlight and a rifle.

"What happened? Where's Charlie?" Sarah demanded to know.

"I—I—" Ethan stopped and then seemed to brace himself. "I yelled at him and he ran off."

Paralyzed for a moment, Sarah couldn't seem to process what she'd just been told. "A rifle?" she asked.

"There are bears and wolves around here," he reminded her, slipping the carrying strap over his shoulder.

Realizing the danger that implied for her son, she said, "Which direction did he head?" Sarah's voice had taken on an icy quality, her tone clipped and precise. Ethan pointed. She grabbed his arm, squeezing hard and warning, "You stay away from my son."

Though she saw the color drain from his cheeks, Ethan's voice was firm as he said, "We have to do this together."

"If anything happens to him..." she warned.

"I know. Don't you think I know what I've done?" he said disconsolately as he spun about and jogged into the woods.

Sarah grabbed Teddy's hand and then softened her manner, explaining that they were going to pack a little bag and then go and find Charlie.

"Are you mad at Ethan, Mommy?" Teddy asked quietly.

"It's nothing you need to worry about, sweetheart," Sarah said. "Let's go find Charlie."

Leaving a trail of string behind them to ensure they wouldn't get lost, Sarah and Teddy searched for Charlie until dark had descended deeply and their voices were hoarse from calling for the little boy. The night air was frosty and Sarah was terrified by the possible effects of the cold on such a little body.

When her arms were numb from carrying Teddy against her shoulder where he slept soundly, Sarah finally retraced her trail of string to the cabin, stripping Teddy down and tucking him into bed. When she didn't find Ethan at the cabin, she assumed he was still searching for Charlie. Deep down she knew he wouldn't stop until he found him.

Wrapping herself in the thick wool blanket from her bed, she stood outside the patio door trying desperately to see into the darkness, hoping and praying that Ethan would find Charlie. As she prayed for Ethan's success, she understood that this incident would change everything between them.

Hours passed and Sarah prayed and prayed for her little son. Finally, as the darkness peaked at midnight, Ethan appeared with a little body in his arms. She could see Charlie's violent shivering from this distance as she opened the patio door to welcome them in.

"He's hypothermic. Get a hot bath ready," Ethan said with no emotion in his voice.

Sarah ran off to follow his instructions, preparing a bath and retrieving Charlie's warmest clothes and then putting on the kettle. By the time she returned to the washroom, Ethan had laid the little boy on the bathmat and was removing his shoes and socks. Seeing his blue lips and toes, Sarah pushed Ethan out of the way without a word and stripped Charlie expertly, placing him carefully in the bath, supporting his head out of the water, the waves rippling from his shivers. Soon the warm water seeped into Charlie's body and his color returned. When he began whimpering and his eyes fluttered, Ethan instructed her to bring him out quickly and wrap him in the thick, warm towel which he held out for her, wrapping Charlie and rubbing his chest and arms and legs. Once Charlie was dry, she dressed him in a t-shirt, flannel pyjamas and socks and then wrapped him in her woolen blanket, holding him tightly against her chest.

Standing back, Ethan was silent except to provide instructions.

"Tea with lots of sugar," he told her. Sarah carried Charlie to the kitchen, cooling the tea from boiling hot to fairly warm with ice cubes that he could drink it as she tipped the mug for him. Consuming about half the cupful, Charlie laid his head against Sarah's shoulder and his eyes drifted closed.

"Now, put him in the bed between us," Ethan said.

Sarah glared at Ethan but he returned her gaze implacably until she moved away to his bedroom, setting Charlie in the middle of the bed. Ethan stripped to his undershorts, pulling long pyjama pants on and a hoodie. Sarah left but soon returned dressed in a similar fashion. She crawled into the bed, loosened the blanket and pulled Charlie against her into the safety of her body. Ethan moved in closely on the other side of Charlie, tucking the wool blanket around mother and son and then wrapping his arms around them protectively, effectively creating a cocoon of warmth for Charlie. Sarah stiffened at Ethan's touch but she didn't remove his arm.

Awaking alone the next morning, Sarah heard her children's voices, both the boys chattering in the lounge. Exiting Ethan's bedroom, she saw him at the stove cooking eggs and bacon as Teddy and Charlie bounced around the furniture playing mountain goats and lava. Moving over to the kitchen area, Sarah poured a cup of coffee pretending to ignore Ethan. In fact, she could see that he was mourning. His eyes were dark and sad and he looked as though he hadn't slept all night. When the boys' breakfasts were finished, he mutely served them up and then walked away to his bedroom without a backward glance. Sarah watched him and then called the boys over.

"So you're feeling better are you, Mr. Charlie Maier?" she asked, keeping her voice light and happy.

"Uh huh. Eefan make baccy eggs!" he replied.

Shaking her head in wonder at how quickly little boys recovered, she watched Teddy and Charlie gobble their breakfasts and then run up to the loft to pull out Teddy's dinosaurs and some of the other toys from Papa Bert's bags. Sarah showered and changed, moving back to the kitchen to make her own breakfast. Showered and dressed, Ethan re-emerged shortly after her, approaching her, opening his mouth to speak. She turned her back on him and walked away.

That's the way the day progressed, that day and the next few. Ethan was silent and mournful and Sarah completely ignored him except when he had the audacity to approach her, at which time she cast him glares of anger and disgust. The little boys soon recognized the tension in the air and stopped speaking to Ethan.

Three days after Charlie ran away, Sarah stood outside the cabin, drinking coffee and looking out over the trees to the mountains beyond as the boys watched cartoons on television. Tensing when she heard the patio door slide further open and then close again without hearing the tell-tale "Mommy!" she assumed it was Ethan.

"Sarah." His voice was gravelly as though the burden of every sorrow in his life had descended upon his vocal chords. Stepping around her, he removed the mug from her hand, but she refused to acknowledge him, continuing to look above him at the clouds. "Sarah, please. Talk to me. Yell at me. I don't care. Slap me—"

The ferocity of her slap knocked him back a step and she saw his cheek glow red from the contact. Rather than rail against him as she expected to do, the words failed her and she stepped into the circle of his embrace, resting her face against his chest, covering her eyes with her hands. He held her close as she cried out her terror and misery.

"You've ruined everything," she cried.

"I know, baby, I know. I'm so sorry," Ethan said.

"How could you?" Her voice faded as her tears took hold again. He held her tightly against him as though he knew he would never again have the privilege and therefore needed to savor every moment. As she began to quiet, she spoke again. "I can't be with you now. I have to put the children's needs first, ahead of my own. I can't have you with them if I can't trust you to keep them safe." She sighed raggedly, despair in her voice. "Unless you're willing to wait eighteen years until they're grown, it's over before it even really began."

Still holding her close with one arm, he tipped her chin to meet his gaze. "I would wait eighteen hundred years for you, sweetheart. Never doubt it. I love you, Sarah."

She groaned loudly. "Now?" she exclaimed indignantly. "Now is the time you choose to tell me that? I can't, Ethan."

She watched the sorrow in his eyes as he replied softly, "I know. I understand. I just thought you should know."

She began to cry again, more softly this time. "What happened?" She emphasized each word.

"I was reading microfilm, a newspaper article on a hit that I've long suspected was perpetrated by Vakh when Charlie woke up and came down. I asked him to get a juice box and color for a few minutes and then we would play together.

He…he wrote in my mother's Bible with his markers." Sarah looked up, astonished. "I…well, I lost it with him. I yelled at him and sent him to sit on the back steps until I could calm down. When I looked out, he was gone. That was just a few minutes before you came back with Teddy. I'm sorry, Sarah. I can think of a million things I should have done but I didn't." He rested his forehead on her shoulder. "I understand why you don't want me around your kids." Kissing her once on the neck, he pulled back, meeting her gaze. "I'll find a safe place for you to go. I give you my word. I'll find a way to get you home."

Hearing the mourning in his voice, Sarah wrapped her arms around his waist, pulling him closer as she wiped her tears across his shirt.

"Mommy?" Teddy called, pushing open the patio door and joining the adults. Hiding her sorrow, Sarah quickly wiped her face with her hands, stepping back from Ethan as Teddy continued. "Charlie says he saw a rabbit."

"That's nice, honey. What are you watching? A nature show?" she asked, sniffing to try and maintain a steady voice.

"No, mommy. The other day. Charlie said he wrote a letter to Ethan in his Bible and then Ethan got mad at him and then he saw a rabbit. He chased it but it got away. He found a cave and he got sleepy," Teddy said.

Stunned by what the boy had said Sarah sought to clarify his statement. "Teddy. Why did Charlie run away?"

"Cause he saw the rabbit," Teddy said.

Sarah looked up at Ethan, her face masked by astonishment. Quickly, she moved into the cabin, calling Charlie over.

"Charlie, the other day when you ran away, what did you write in Ethan's Bible," Sarah said.

"I wuf you," Charlie replied.

"I love you, too, son. But what did you write?" she said.

"I show you." Charlie ran into Ethan's room and returned with the brown leather book. "See?" He opened the book to

Leviticus, pointing out the green marker swirls across the page. "I-wuf-you, Eefan."

"Did Ethan get mad at you?" Sarah asked.

"Uh huh," Charlie replied calmly. "Pensoh. No marker," he said very seriously, indicating his belief that Ethan's angry response stemmed from the fact that he had written using markers rather than a pencil.

She gasped. "Why did you run away?"

"Bunny hop hop hop. Bunny gone. Me so seepy. Eefan find me," Charlie said.

Charlie and Teddy skipped away, back to the television.

"Sarah?" Ethan placed a story of questions within her name, hope in his voice.

She turned her eyes to him in wonder. *Charlie didn't run away because of Ethan's behavior. He simply wanted to see the rabbit. True, Ethan didn't watch him as closely as he should have but he must have been very upset to see his mother's Bible marked like that. He could have overreacted in so many ways but he didn't. He recognized that he needed to be calm to deal with Charlie. Oh, Father, does that mean that I can trust him, that it's okay for me to fall in love with Ethan Lange?*

A warm glow filled Sarah's heart and she threw her arms around the man who had successfully worked his way into the hearts of her sons, and her own as well. "Oh, Ethan. Forgive me?"

He held her tightly until she released him and then trapped her face in his hands. "There's nothing to forgive. Give me another chance? I promise I won't fail you again, beautiful Sarah."

Tenderly, she ran her fingers through his curly blonde hair, stroking his cheeks with the palms of her hands. "How did this happen between us, Ethan?" she asked. He shrugged in response.

"I wasn't looking for love," he said, mimicking her and she laughed.

"Maybe I was wrong," she said.

He swept her up in his arms. They laughed and kissed and laughed some more as the weight of sorrow was lifted from their hearts and the lightness of what just might become love took its place.

CHAPTER 16

IA officer, Ronald McCreary paced behind the Deputy Director's desk, his attention now on Isabella Farini and Owen Alastair Cullen who tensed for the battle to come.

"Agent Cullen, how long have you worked for Lange's team?" McCreary said.

"Two years, sir. He's a brilliant agent," Owen said.

McCreary leaned forward, threat in his very posture. "When I want your opinion Cullen, I'll give it to you." Owen blushed at the demeaning tone. McCreary shifted his attention to Bella. "Ms. Farini, on the day of Senator Tom Baker's murder, what were you doing?"

"Our team arrived in response to the 911 call which was routed to us because of the suspicion of terrorism," Bella said. "Special Agent Jack Dietrich ordered Owen and myself to pursue the two gunmen who escaped by car."

"Did you apprehend them?" McCreary said.

"No, sir. The gunmen disappeared. We chased them for a dozen blocks and then they just vanished," Bella said.

"Where was Ethan Lange during this time?" McCreary asked.

"Dietrich sent him after Vakh," Bella said.

McCreary frowned. "And we all know what happened then. Mr. Lange's abilities were unquestionably lacking. If the two of you hope to salvage your careers after such a blunder, you had better come up with more useful information than this." Leaning on his forearms, his intense gaze held them as he shifted from the months' old assassination of the senator to the present troubles. "Where is Ethan Lange and who is the witness he's protecting?"

Sarah watched Ethan from where she leaned against the kitchen wall. He was hunched over the laptop again. He spent hours every day at it, reading and scribbling away on a pad of paper, determined to solve the puzzle of Bibi Baker and Borz Vakh. Intent as he was, though, when Teddy burst in through the patio door with a handful of bugs, Ethan took the time to examine them and hear all the chatter the little boy offered. And then he admonished Teddy not to eat too many before lunch. Incredulous, Teddy laughed, denying any interest in a snack of insects before rejoining Charlie in the dirt just outside the patio door.

Suddenly, Sarah couldn't resist Ethan any longer. Moving closer, she wrapped her arms around his shoulders and kissed him on the cheek.

"I wondered how long you were going to ogle me," Ethan said, a smile in his eyes.

Slapping him lightly on the shoulder, she denied the accusation. "I wasn't ogling you. Just watching…and appreciating."

Turning on the high stool, he pulled her close. "And ogling me," he said.

She laughed. "Okay, maybe I was ogling you a bit."

"Thought so."

Kissing her deeply, he reluctantly pulled away when Charlie burst in with the bestest stone ever to be found.

Ethan chuckled. "This is what your life is like, isn't it?"

She smiled, pulling him back into a hug. "Yeah. Still interested?"

"More than I ever imagined."

She brushed her fingers through his curls. "Why do you keep your hair so short? You have the cutest curls."

Snorting indignantly, he subconsciously ran his fingers over his scalp. "Not exactly a characteristic that terrorists respect."

Sarah laughed, taking a seat on the high stool beside him. She picked up the pad of paper on the counter, reading through his notes.

"So, the popular senator Tom Baker had an affair three years ago," she said. "Interesting."

"Yes. And there seems to have been some kind of back room dealing which finally convinced Bibi to stick around rather than kick her husband out on his ear, effectively ending his political career. Johnny found evidence that she was offered a run at a local seat in government but then the powers-that-be reneged leaving Bibi with the humiliation but no reward," Ethan said.

"How did Johnny come by that kind of information?" Sarah asked, suspicious of her friend's questionable methods.

"I'm not certain but it sounds like a motive for murder to me," Ethan said.

"But how does Borz Vakh figure in all of this?" Sarah said.

"Shortly after you and I left Washington, Bella deposited some information in a dummy website we've used in the past. I only found it a couple of days ago. It shows that Vakh was brought into the country on an Irish passport on a private jet leased to a company owned by…" Ethan paused to let her fill in the blanks.

"Tom Baker?" Sarah said.

"Better. Bibi herself. She is independently wealthy through an inheritance from her maternal grandfather. I guess she's used to having her cake and eating it too," he said.

"Okay, so let me understand this. Bibi is linked to Vakh. She has motive and means," Sarah said.

"I also contacted my brother, Stevie. He's a police detective just like my father. I asked him to call in some favors and trace back the 911 recording that brought the FBI to the site of the terror attack. It was made by the wife of Bibi's chauffeur," Ethan said.

"That's a lot of links added to what Johnny said about her announcing her bid for senate on the day your enquiry began. Do you have enough proof?" Sarah said.

"Not really. Not yet," he replied.

"She's also rather sloppy, don't you think, leaving clues all over the place?" Sarah said.

"Sloppy or very, very confident," Ethan said.

"What about the Marines? You said the fellow that showed up at the safe house in Washington wearing the green suit might have been in the Marines?" Sarah said.

"Tom Baker was a Marine. It's tenuous, but I'm assuming that would afford Bibi with the connections she needed to enlist an ex-Marine into service, particularly if I could confirm the rumor that she had an affair with a fellow officer," Ethan said.

"Hmmm. That would be suspicious. Ethan, you've never told me exactly what happened the day Vakh escaped," Sarah said.

"I'll tell you chronologically though I've only just recently realized the connections between these events. Six months ago, our unit started hearing rumblings of a new terrorist threat targeting some of our politicians. There was the bombing of a pub well-known to be frequented by young eligible senators, which led to the death of an aid and the injury of two junior senators. Next there was the bombing attempt on the off-site hearings of the Bureau of Indian Affairs task force. Believing this to be a new terror campaign, my unit was called in to investigate and compile a plan to infiltrate the terrorist cell and dismantle it. I was due to go undercover but the bomb at the hearings occurred while we were still in the planning stage," Ethan said.

"Tom Baker?" Sarah said.

"Was amongst the group of senators at the pub and sat on the Indian Affairs task force. There was no threat made to Baker directly so no one realized that he was the keystone to the investigation. Four months ago…" Ethan checked the date on his watch. "Almost five months ago, a 911 call came through to us, flagged because the caller used the words, 'terrorist attack' and mentioned the presence of public officials. Because my team had been in the middle of a planning meeting, we all responded. Arriving, we witnessed three masked gunmen backing out of the building. Two of the gunmen escaped in a black Chevy that Dietrich sent Owen and Bella to pursue. The third gunman ran toward the city park where he was apprehended by regular FBI. I entered the building under Dietrich's orders discovering Vakh in a conference room with FBI agent Werner Smith. Vakh turned his gun on Smith." Ethan faltered at the conflict the memory always evoked in his conscience.

"I'm listening," Sarah encouraged him quietly to continue. "But just for future reference, in case I forget to mention this, it sounds to me like Werner Smith should have been reprimanded for carelessness. I mean, how did he let Vakh get the drop on him?"

"Hmm," Ethan murmured thoughtfully and then continued, "Vakh backed out of the room using Smith as a human shield. I let him escape rather than jeopardize Smith's life." Ethan paused, taking a deep breath as though bracing himself. "There were police officers and FBI agents including CAUDO agents everywhere but somehow Vakh escaped. There were a few more gunshots and then Baker was found dead. It was assumed that Vakh had shot Baker after I had released him. As a consequence, I was blamed for the death."

Sarah finally understood. "He was already dead, wasn't he?"

"I think so. I believe that Bibi Baker hired Vakh to murder her husband as revenge for his public infidelity. Her political campaign is loaded with references to the untimely death of her husband and her own bereavement and the impetus that event has given her to *stand for the people*."

"What does the attack on the National Gallery have to do with any of this?" Sarah asked.

"The Chairman of the Party—you know, the fellow who offered Bibi political office and then reneged? Well, he was visiting the gallery that day with his family, incognito. I believe that she wanted to restore her own public and, likely, private image. If she'd already gotten away with the murder of her husband, it stands to reason, that she would try again," Ethan said.

"How much can you prove?" Sarah said.

"Not enough. Not yet. And without solid proof, they'll just ship me off to prison and eliminate me at their earliest convenience," he said.

"Oh, Ethan sweetheart. What are we going to do?" she said, reaching for his hand.

He smiled at her, the happy smile that made her tummy do a flip-flop. "I like it when you include me in that *we*," he said.

She kissed him lightly on the mouth but he kissed her deeply, cradling her head in the palm of his hand. And she was lost in the sensation of mouth, his body warm against hers. When he pulled back, he rested his forehead against hers for a long moment.

When he finally spoke, he said, "Short of forcing a confession out of Bibi or Vakh, I'm not certain. Keep digging, I guess."

"Or, you could take us on a picnic by the lake," Sarah said.

He frowned thoughtfully, tapping a finger against his chin. "Better idea," he muttered and then grinned. "If you gather a blanket and a few toys and books, I'll make some sandwiches."

"That sounds wonderful," she said. She kissed him on the cheek calling out to the boys to wash up and assist in her search for the perfect picnic blanket.

After feasting on the sandwiches and apples, Ethan, Sarah and the boys engaged in an all-holds-barred game of football with the ball that Ethan had rescued from his father's attic back home. After the rough-and-tumble of the game, Charlie pulled Ethan over to the blanket for a story.

Returning from escorting Teddy to an appropriate tree to relieve himself, Sarah smiled fondly at the sight before her. Ethan was lying on his back fast asleep on the blanket, one arm tucked behind his head and one arm around Charlie who was sleeping against his chest.

Sarah suggested an *explore* and she and Teddy trooped around the lake and then into a stand of brilliant climbing trees. Hoisting Teddy onto a low branch, Sarah found a second perch a few trees away and they played pirates and giants until Sarah began to feel it was time to return to Ethan and Charlie.

As they wandered back through the forest, Sarah heard an odd huffing sound. Emerging from the trees, Sarah scanned the area around the lake. She felt a cold wave wash through her. There was a huge grizzly bear standing tall on its hind legs.

"Teddy!" She called back over her shoulder. "Don't come out of the trees. Teddy, can you hear me?"

"Yes, Mommy...but I can find you."

"No!" Her voice was too sharp. She didn't want to frighten Teddy, only ensure his compliance. Blowing out a breath, she tried for a calmer tone of voice. "There is a bear out here but I don't think he's seen you yet. Do you remember how to get back to Ethan?"

"Ye-yes," Teddy said.

"Stay in the trees for as long as you can and run back to Ethan. Tell him to bring the rifle." Her fear escaped into her voice as urgency. "Hurry, Teddy!"

The next thing she heard was a little boy crashing through the brush. Very loudly. Her heart beat a tattoo of fear. The bear only cocked its head to the side, staring directly at Sarah. At the moment it didn't seem agitated. *Lord, I could really use some help. Please send Ethan. Protect Teddy and Charlie. Please.*

It seemed like an eternity before Sarah heard Ethan's voice behind and to the side of her.

"Are you hurt?" he asked, calling to her.

"No. So far he's just curious. What do I do?" she said.

"Stay still. I'll line up a shot." Ethan's voice was steady and calm and Sarah drew comfort from him.

"The boys?" she said.

"Up a tree behind me," he said.

Abruptly, the bear dropped to all fours and cold panic washed through Sarah. But rather than charge, the animal turned its profile to her. Along with the relief she felt at the lessened ursine threat level, she blanched in recognition of the sheer size of the creature.

"I think he's preparing to leave," Ethan reassured her. "Don't—"

A dog barreled out of the trees across the space between Sarah and the grizzly bear, splashing into the lake. Somehow the appearance of the dog had redirected the grizzly's attention to Sarah. Huffing and barking, the grizzly met her gaze, its ears flattened against its head.

"Ethan!" she cried, terror seizing her.

"Don't move, baby! I've got him." She heard his words and felt the edge of her terror retreat enough to allow room for her to keep breathing.

Out from the trees proceeded a high-pitched whistle which seemed to irritate the bear further. It barked once and beat its front paws on the ground. Two young men stepped out of the forest, clearly tourists given their dress and reckless ignorance. Calling the errant canine, they clearly didn't notice the bear.

"Stop where you are!" Ethan called to the boisterous young men.

The dog sank into a crouch, growling at the bear. "What's going on? Buster! Buster, c'mere," the one man called, the one clad in what looked like plaid pyjama pants and a flannel bush jacket. The other man was wearing torn jeans, a Mega-Deth sweatshirt and carrying a bottle in one hand. The growling dog began barking at the sound of his master's voice, creeping closer to the bear.

"Get back! You're in my sights!" Ethan said, shouting at the young men. They didn't seem to understand, moving as they did, closer to their dog…and closer to the grizzly bear.

And then the bear's attention shifted from Sarah directly to the dog.

"Sarah, run to me!" Ethan yelled to her.

Immediately, Sarah spun, slipping on the turf but maintaining her momentum as she ran directly at Ethan, seeing him for the first time, hunting rifle pointing directly over her shoulder. He stood with his back to the sun and she couldn't read his face but saw his body as the haven of safety she desired. Behind Sarah a growling and barking erupted but Ethan urged her onward until she was captured at his side, his one arm tightly around her as his other hand held the rifle at his side.

"Baby, sweetheart, are you okay?" he asked, speaking directly into her ear, his breath puffing against her cheek. She could feel his anxiety mixing with her own breathless fear.

The growling changed to yelping and screaming and Sarah spun to see one of the men throwing stones at the bear to shift its morbid intent from the dog. Her chest squeezed. They couldn't stand by as the bear killed the man.

"Get off!" the man screamed. The second man seemed to be paralyzed in fear until he suddenly decided on action, running back the way he'd come.

"Ethan, that bear is going to kill him. Help him," she said urgently. Shoving her behind him, Ethan set up a shot.

"Get out of the way!" he yelled but the man didn't move. Ethan jogged a few steps forward, leaving Sarah behind, as he muttered, "I can't get a clean shot. If I wound him, it'll only make things worse."

Sarah watched in horror as the man's stone-throwing idiocy finally turned the bear's attention away from his bloody triumph over the canine. The grizzly charged.

"Ethan!" she cried and he took off at a run, directly at the bear, stopping long enough to set up his shot and fire. The bear lurched as the bullet hit him but continued to charge. Ethan cocked the rifle and fired again. This time the bear stopped his charge, moaning, and turned to limp away. Ethan raced after it, trying one more shot but the wounded bear lumbered out of range.

"Hey, man, why didn't you shoot it before it ate my dog? What's wrong with you?"

Ethan's restraint burst and he strode to the man, lifting him bodily by his shirt, drawing him threateningly close to his face.

"You idiot! I saved your life. You could have been the one eaten. Because of your stupidity, there is now a wounded grizzly bear roaming the countryside. You are luckier than you deserve. Get out of my sight!" Ethan dropped him in disgust and strode back to Sarah pulling her tightly into his arms, hugging her fiercely. She held him tightly in return until he finally released her, taking her hand and walking back toward Teddy and Charlie.

"Teddy! Charlie!" Sarah called, desperate to hear their voices, to be assured of their safety.

"I'm here, Mommy," Teddy returned her call.

"Me, Mama!" Charlie said.

Sarah located them, high in a tree, catching them as they dropped into her arms and then pulling Teddy back against her.

"You saved my life, Teddy David," she said. "Thank you."

Teddy smiled grandly and hugged her. All the way back to the cabin, he recounted the entire adventure with Charlie piping in from time. Sarah set him straight, refining the details for Ethan's benefit but Ethan remained silent, holding Sarah's hand tightly, and she wondered that he didn't have more to say.

As Sarah settled the boys with paper and crayons, Ethan retreated to the shed where they'd parked old Jimmy. Lifting the hood on the old truck, Ethan spread out his tools hoping to lose himself in tinkering with the engine. The weight of the promise he'd made, however, drove him to his knees; the promise that he'd made at his first primal reaction to Sarah's danger.

"God. God, what do I do?" Ethan dropped his head onto his arms where they rested against the bumper of the old truck. When Teddy had returned, waking him, telling him that Sarah was being attacked by a bear, Ethan's life had narrowed to one thought, *God, I'll do anything if you save her for me and the boys.*

Now that he'd returned and Sarah and Teddy and Charlie were safe inside his grandfather's cabin, the weight of his offer settled on his shoulders. He shuddered under the burden. *God, when I was a boy I asked you to save my mother but you didn't. Today I asked you to save Sarah and you did. I don't know what to think. I don't know how to feel. I don't know what it all means.* Ethan buried his head in his hands, groaning with the agony of indecision. *If I give in to you, do I have to agree that it was okay for my mother to die? It wasn't okay. It changed my life forever!*

Though trials should come, let this blest assurance control, that Christ has regarded my helpless estate and has shed his own blood for my soul. Horatio Spafford's words filtered through Ethan's mind and then gentled into the tender voice of his mother. His mother holding him close, singing to him as they waited together for help to arrive, trapped in the truck in the irrigation ditch those many years ago. And once again Ethan was a seven year old boy, a tender-hearted boy who dearly loved and was loved by his mother.

"Remember, sweetheart," she'd said. *"Jesus loves you. When you cry for me, Ethan, remember that God reaches down His hand to hold onto yours. I love you, Ethan."*

Ethan was lovable. His mother had loved him. If the words she'd given him were true, then God loved him, too. The heart-deep damage which had resulted from his father's bitterness had hardened Ethan's heart to that love but little Charlie's love had cracked the hardness of Ethan's heart. The more time he spent with Charlie and Teddy and Sarah, the more pliant his heart became and Ethan realized that Charlie had delivered Jesus in the simple faith of a child. The decision really wasn't so difficult after all.

Sarah went in search of Ethan, finding him under the hood of old Jimmy, tinkering and clanging. Calling his name first as a warning of her approach, just in case he was still in action-man mode, she tapped his back when he didn't respond.

"Are you okay?" she asked.

Grunting, Ethan withdrew his head from the engine, wiping his hands on a rag. Leaning back on the vehicle, he met her gaze silently and then reached for her, pulling her close to stand between his knees, his hands on her hips.

"Not really. No," he said. His voice was oddly harsh.

"Oh," she replied, confused by his expression. There was an odd mix of fierceness and gentleness in his manner.

"You wandered off with one of the children without taking the rifle or the bear spray or even telling me where you were going—" he said and she could clearly see the fierceness taking over his expression.

She pressed her fingers to his lips, cutting him off. "All right. I'm sorry. I'm not used to the dangers here. You know, one of these days I'm going to take you home to Whistler—that's in the mountains of British Columbia—and then just see how much sympathy you get from me when the frostbite sets in," she said ironically.

His posture relaxed and a grin pulled at the corner of his mouth. He blew out a breath. "You scared the snot out of me." All humour dropped from his expression and he pulled her close, holding her just a bit too tight.

Concerned, she asked him, "Ethan? Sweetheart? What's wrong?"

"I only wounded the bear. He's much more dangerous now than before. I'll have to report it," he said.

Was that why he was so concerned? The wounded bear? Or the reporting of the incident? "You could go into town and call anonymously from a pay phone," she suggested, trying to sound optimistic.

"I intend to but shooting a bear out of season requires an investigation. If those young idiots tell the tale and I do not doubt that they will…well…" He gestured widely.

Now she understood. "This could lead the bad guys to our door?" she said.

"Yes," he replied.

"We can't put other people at risk to protect ourselves," she said. "We have to tell."

"I know," he said.

"Things will change now, won't they?" she said.

"Yes."

She sighed sadly. "I've kind of gotten used to the way things are." Wrapping her arms around his shoulders, she held on tight.

CHAPTER 17

Avoiding the surveillance cameras, Ethan parked beneath a large, leafy tree in the farthest corner of the parking lot of the Pitkin Post Office. Exiting the vehicle, Ethan lifted Teddy down beside him, taking his hand. They found the public telephone right outside the front entrance.

"Ethan, can we call Grandpa?" Teddy asked.

"Not this time, pal," Ethan said.

"Can we get some ice cream?" Teddy pointed back the way they'd come. "I saw a great big ice cream cone over there." Optimistically, he looked up into Ethan's eyes.

"Can we talk about it after I make this call, honey?" Ethan said, knowing he sounded as grim as he felt.

"Okay," Teddy replied seriously, clearly absorbing the tension in Ethan's manner.

Wondering if it had been a mistake to give in to the boy's pleading to come along, Ethan added that worry to his anxiety about the risk he was taking by reporting the bear attack. But how could he not? A wounded grizzly could put many others at risk.

"Stay right here with me, okay, Teddy?" Ethan requested. Nodding, Teddy tucked the fingers of his free hand into Ethan's belt, his nonverbal promise not to wander off. Plugging in the requisite coins, Ethan dialed the number of the local rangers.

"*Open Space and Mountain Parks Department.*"

Ethan sighed. "I'd like to report a wounded grizzly bear."

"Where and when was the sighting?"

"Yesterday afternoon," Ethan said. "Nine miles southwest of Pitkin. It was heading due north."

"Thank you, sir. Could you—"

Ethan ended the call. That would give the Game Wardens enough to go on without adding undue risk to Sarah and the boys. If the FBI was watching alerts nationwide and heard of the shooting…once they eventually realized his connection to the cabin and, if they put two and two together…well, four was a nice round number to work with…well, rather angular and straight, actually. If Vakh and Bibi were watching? So much the worse.

Taking Teddy's hand again and thanking him for waiting, Ethan walked back toward the Jimmy. The boisterous activities of a group of young tourists coming out of the liquor store across the parking lot caught his attention.

"Hey!"

Tugging Teddy along with him, Ethan ignored the man hollering and pointing at them. As the jogging footsteps approached, Ethan lifted Teddy into his arms, ready to defend the boy by any and all means.

"Hey! You're the guy who got the bear!"

No, this can't be happening. "Teddy, when I put you down, I want you to run and get in the truck. Understand?" Ethan said.

"Yes," Teddy whispered his solemn word.

"Hey, guys, c'mere. This is the guy I told you about. He killed my dog!"

"Now!" Ethan dropped Teddy to his feet and the boy took off, struggling for a moment with the door and then managing to squeeze in and pull it shut. "Lock it!" Ethan called to him and Teddy complied, locking all the doors. Now Ethan turned his attention to the men bearing down on him, five guys, between nineteen and twenty-four years of age, agitated and reasonably fit. Ethan groaned. *God? I could use a little help. Please?*

The five men fanned out in front of Ethan, looking like a set of bowling pins and Ethan wondered, if he could just manage to tip the first fellow over, would the others fall as well?

"You killed my dog!" the young man accused.

"You killed your dog. Didn't you read the signs that warned you to keep pets under control?" Ethan retorted.

Surveying the group, Ethan quickly devised a plan of attack that would hopefully leave him still standing and able to drive Teddy back to the cabin unharmed. *Why did I let Teddy come? I'll never forgive myself if he's hurt.*

"Why you—" The dog owner began and then dropped his bottle on the ground and charged at Ethan, swinging a haymaker toward his jaw. Sidestepping easily, Ethan punched him in the temple with his fisted car keys and dog owner fell like a stone. Growling in fury, two more charged and Ethan decided to take the punch from the smaller guy, twisting so the man's fist connected directly with his shoulder. The man yelped in pain, clutching his broken wrist against his chest. Without a moment's pause, Ethan fisted the other man's shirt, pulling him forward into his knee, winding him.

Turning to the last two men standing, Ethan paced forward and then stood, legs shoulder width apart, hands fisted. The other men retreated, hands in the air in surrender. Ethan quickly took advantage of their reluctance, jogging to the truck and unlocking the door with his key, stepping in and keying the ignition while commanding Teddy to do up his seatbelt. Dropping the gearshift into reverse, he backed swiftly out of the parking space, turning onto the main road out of town as he did up his own seatbelt.

The post office. There were security cameras everywhere. *If old Jimmy is spotted on the surveillance cameras, we're toast.* If not, surely the idiot tourists would report him to the local sheriff and that would have the same result. He needed a new plan.

"You were tough," Teddy said, clearly awed by the spectacle he'd just seen.

Ethan desperately wanted to make Teddy promise not to tell Sarah about the altercation but he knew that would be wrong. He'd have to face the consequences of her anger and hope and pray that she wouldn't cast him aside.

"Teddy?" Ethan said.

"Uh-huh," Teddy replied.

"Do you know how to pray?" Ethan asked.

"Sure," Teddy said, full of confidence. "I say my prayers every night and we ask the blessing every time we eat."

"How do I pray that Mommy won't be mad at me for fighting?" Ethan asked.

"Just ask God to help you tell her. He always listens. Mommy says He doesn't always give us what we want but He always loves us," Teddy proudly conveyed the information, quoting his mother carefully.

"Thanks buddy." Ethan rested his hand on Teddy's shoulder for a moment. "I'm kind of new at this stuff."

"Ethan, did you ask Jesus into your heart?" Teddy asked.

"Er, yes, I guess I did," Ethan replied.

"Cool! Me, too," Teddy said. "Ethan, do you love Mommy?"

Surprised at first, Ethan's wide-eyed shock quickly morphed into a grin. "Yes." When or how it had happened he wasn't certain but just the thought of life without Sarah was unacceptable.

"Me too," Teddy said cheerfully. "She's the greatest."

"Yes, honey, she is the greatest," Ethan said. Now if he could just make her fall in love with him.

Teddy patted Ethan's knee sympathetically. "Don't worry. Mommy will forgive you for fighting."

"Thanks." Ethan paused, a small smile escaping. "Teddy? I love you, too."

Teddy grinned broadly. "Me, too."

The rest of the journey passed in silence until they entered the laneway.

"Ethan!" Teddy exclaimed, astounded.

"What Teddy?" Ethan replied, very concerned at the boy's demeanor.

"We forgot to get ice cream!" Teddy groaned in dismay.

Ethan snorted and then chuckled. "Oh no! Do you think we could convince mommy to make us some cookies instead?"

Teddy clapped his hands at the idea. "Yes yes! We won't tell her about the fight…" His eyes fell. "Wait. We gotta tell her, don't we?"

Ethan remembered his earlier doubts about a confession, sighing. "Yes. What if you let me tell her?"

"Okay. You tell her and I'll ask for cookies," Teddy said. "Deal?"

Pulling the truck into the shed, Ethan turned to Teddy, extending his hand. "Deal." They shook on it and it was settled.

Bracing themselves with unison deep breaths, Teddy and Ethan entered the cabin, greeted by Charlie.

"Home! Come see," Charlie said.

"Mommy!" Teddy hollered and Sarah dashed out of the washroom, her hands still dripping.

"Yes, Teddy! What happened?" she gasped.

Calmly, he asked, "Could you please make us some cookies 'cause we didn't get to stop for ice cream?"

She laughed outright. "Yes, I will make you cookies." She laughed again until she met Ethan's gaze and quickly sobered. "Teddy, why don't you take Charlie into my room and jump on the bed for a while?"

"Yeah!"

"Hurray!"

Ethan wanted to pull her close but was still uncertain of her reaction to the news he brought. So he kept his distance, not afraid of her smacking him again, just not wanting to see her anger up close if it was going to be directed at him.

"Ethan, what happened?" she asked, her eyes squinting. "What are you reluctant to tell me?"

Astonished at her insight, he ducked his head like a little boy expecting a well-deserved reprimand. Recognizing his reaction, he forced himself to meet her gaze. He no longer had the excuse of youth. "I'm not particularly fond of making you angry with me," he said.

"Have you betrayed me?" she asked, taking a step toward him.

"No."

"The children?" she asked, stepping closer. He inhaled deeply, drawing in the essence of *Sarah*: sweetness, kindness and baby powder.

"No, Sarah."

"Do you love me?" she said.

Her hands were on him, stroking up his chest and across his shoulders and he lost the feeling of being a child as the now familiar longing raced along his nerves. His voice dropped two tones and he felt her shudder in response. "Yes, you know I do," he murmured against her.

"Do you know that I love you?" she asked as she leaned against him.

Her mouth was suddenly very near his own and he was mesmerized by her soft, inviting lips, those lips that kissed away his fears and anxieties and told him a story of love. "No. Do you?"

"Yes." She breathed the word against his mouth.

"Good." His lungs pumped like he was running a race.

Bracing her hands on his shoulders, she pulled away, shrugging playfully, "Then I'm not sure what the problem is."

His arms wound around her waist, drawing her close again, not willing to lose the moment. "Me neither," he murmured, kissing her.

When he pulled back, her eyes fluttered slowly open. "The young idiots were there," he said, his voice still breathy. "I had to fight them. Broke a wrist and a couple of ribs."

Shocked, she pulled back, lifting his shirt. "Where? Your wrist?"

"Not mine. Theirs," he said, lifting her chin to place a gentle kiss on her lips.

"Oh." She sighed. "I shouldn't be relieved by that I suppose, but I am. Teddy?"

"He was perfect, Sarah. I told him to run to the truck and get in and he did, locking all the doors," Ethan said. "It's only a matter of time now, sweetheart. That, and whether Vakh finds us before the FBI," he said.

She clung tightly to him, saying, "The FBI would be better, wouldn't it?"

"Probably, but not definitely. CAUDO is not going to let me walk away from this," he said.

"Ethan, I don't want you to go to prison and I don't want you to die. What are our best options to just get you fired?" she said.

He laughed aloud. "I'm not sure if that makes you an optimist or a pessimist."

"I don't really care. Should we call Johnny?" she said.

He nodded and then shook his head. "If I can gather enough evidence, I could turn myself in. Until then, I have to stay free." Ethan began to pace. "I wish I could talk to my father. Perhaps he'd know what to do."

"You could call him," she suggested. "The satellite phone is clean."

"Yes, but my father's phone is probably bugged. You know, I've wished a hundred times through the years that I could go to my father for advice, times when there was too much anger and disappointment between us. Now that I could finally go to him, I can't," Ethan said, grimly admitting the irony.

"I'll call Johnny," she said.

"No. *I'll* call Johnny," Ethan said. "You need to get together a bag for the boys; a bag with their passports and a letter to give my father permission to take them across the border. They'll need clothes and toys and snacks."

"Why your father?" she asked, furrowing her brow.

"Johnny says that you and I are on a watch list at the border but the boys aren't listed. Would you trust my father with them?" he asked.

"Yes, I think so. But where would he take them?" she said.

"To your father?" Ethan said.

"Okay," she responded hesitantly.

"Is that a good place for them to wait for you?" Ethan asked, now concerned about the assumptions he'd made.

Smiling, she replied, "Yes. Dad would take very good care of them."

Resting his hand on her shoulder, he tenderly asked, "Sarah, what happened to your mother? I've only ever heard you mention her once."

Sarah's eyes filled with tears. "She died two months after David. I...I felt so alone. My mother was my best friend and just when I needed her the most, she was gone."

Taking her hands, he kissed them both and then placed them against his chest, holding them there. "Is that why love hurts you so much?"

Nodding, one stray tear fell along her cheek. He watched it fall, catching it with his thumb as she explained, "It's easier just to focus on the three of us. It's exhausting and consuming and then I don't have to feel the loss so much. If I assume I have no help, I don't expect it and then I can't be disappointed."

"How do you deal with all of this—" He gestured around them. "Heartache?"

"God. 'Trust in the Lord with all your heart and lean not on your own understanding. In all your ways acknowledge Him and He will direct your paths'," Sarah quoted her favorite verse. "When we take Jesus as our Saviour, we become associated with God and, therefore, have access to his care and protection."

"Sarah, when you were facing that grizzly bear, I prayed, asking God to save you so I could get to know you better and get to know Him better. That's what I was doing in the shed with old Jimmy afterwards. I let God in and asked Him to take over my life," Ethan said.

A wide, happy smile spread across Sarah's face. "So that's what happened! Your behavior was very odd. But I'm so happy, Ethan. Has it made you feel any different?"

"There was no lightning bolt or anything and I don't really understand what it all means but it brought back that same feeling I remember as a little boy sitting in my mother's arms. Peace. I feel more at peace about a lot of things," Ethan said.

Wrapping her arms around his waist, Sarah leaned her head against his chest. He let her rest against him for a moment and then held her away from him, stepping over to get the satellite phone.

Before he activated it, she asked, "You're thinking of a plan?"

"Yes. It's not ideal but it should work to get you and Teddy and Charlie to safety," he said.

"What about you?" she asked.

"I don't know, Sarah. I may have only delayed the inevitable," he admitted.

"No, Ethan. I'm not leaving while you're still in danger," she said.

Moved by her care for him, he stepped closer, cradling her face in his hands. "Sarah, my darling, I never expected to have someone like you love me. If all I can have of life is these few weeks we've had together, it will be enough." Resting his cheek against hers, he said gruffly, "Tell me you love me, baby."

"I love you. Teddy and Charlie love you. But Ethan, it's not enough for me. I gave my heart to one man and he broke it. Please don't break my heart again," she said.

"I can't promise. But I can promise to love you all my life, Sarah," Ethan said. "And I promise you that if there is any breath in my body or life in my limbs that I will come for you."

"Ethan, I need you to make me one more promise," Sarah said.

"Anything," he said, urging her to continue.

"If you ever have to choose between my life and the boys', I want you to promise that you will save them first," she said.

He shook his head vigorously. "I won't make that choice. There's always a third option."

Clinging to his shirt, she begged him, "Please, Ethan. Please, promise me."

Finally, he nodded. "I promise. But then I'm coming for you."

She nodded as well. "Yes. That's good enough," she said, her voice shaky and low.

"Johnny," Ethan said. He needed Johnny Parsons to be trustworthy, so Ethan trusted him. For Sarah's sake. "I need you to do me a favor," Ethan continued, not bothering with a greeting. "Hire the best lawyer you can afford and get him here to represent Sarah. I'll pay you back as soon as I'm out of this mess."

For a moment, all Ethan heard was static over the satellite phone until, finally, Johnny replied. "What about the kids?"

"I've got a plan for them," Ethan said.

"Right," Johnny replied. "I checked with my sources at the Canada-U.S. border and there's still no alert on Teddy and Charlie. I tried to get my buddy to lose the alert on Sarah but there was no chance."

That hope faded. "Thanks for trying," Ethan said.

"You're going to need a good lawyer as well, man," Johnny said.

"I don't care about myself, Johnny. If Sarah and the kids are safe, I'll find a way to cope," Ethan said.

"Fine. Look after my Sarah," Johnny said with warning in his voice.

"I'll look after *my* Sarah," Ethan replied. "You go and get your own."

Johnny laughed loudly down the phone line. "Hey, I tried once, man, but she wouldn't have me." Johnny disconnected.

Next Ethan called his father but there was no answer and he didn't dare leave a message. There was nothing left to do but wait. They were on their way, Vakh, the FBI, maybe even the Marines if Bibi had her way. *I certainly hope that God is in control.*

CHAPTER 18

"Just a little further," Ethan informed his little posse. "Teddy, how many oak trees from the edge of the meadow?"

"Eight," the boy announced proudly from his perch on his mother's back.

"Very good!" Ethan praised him, reaching over to ruffle Teddy's sandy brown hair. "Charlie, where do we turn?"

"Big wock!" Charlie said, bouncing up and down excitedly on Ethan's shoulders. Ethan tightened his grip on the little boy's ankles to keep him in place.

"Now," Ethan said. "We go around the snake rocks and..." He paused, setting the two boys on their feet, before continuing, "We push aside these bushes and crawl inside." Unclipping the flashlight from his belt, Ethan led the way and Sarah brought up the rear.

This labyrinth of caves had been Ethan's favorite retreat when he was a boy, a safe haven from his brothers' teasing and his father's disappointment. The summer after Ethan's eleventh birthday, he and his grandfather had carved out a cavern, supplying it with all manner of provisions. A person could survive for weeks in there perfectly safely. And Ethan knew the tunnel system well enough to climb right through the mountain if necessary. They could hide or escape as needed.

Pulling out the toys and supplies that they'd brought today, Ethan showed the boys the boundaries of safe play and then pulled Sarah to sit beside him on a ledge of rock that he had used as a bed once during a camp-out with his grandfather.

Leaning into his side, Sarah asked, "Are you sure this is the best way?"

Ethan nodded, pulling out the hand-drawn map he'd made. "Yes. No one ever found me here," he said, tracing the route through the mountain. "We can work our way out of here to the other side of the mountain at Crested Butte, cross the Gunnison National Forest and escape via the old highway."

"What if...what if we get separated?" she asked and her voice trembled at the idea.

"You bring the boys here and I come for you," he replied simply.

"That's easy to say but—"

"I will come for you, Sarah." Tracing her jaw with his fingertips, he turned her face to him, kissing her once. "You and Teddy and Charlie mean everything to me."

"Okay," she replied, grasping his shirt in her fists. "Okay."

Picking flowers with the boys at the edge of the roadway, Sarah was startled to see a blue Ford Focus turning their way. Calling the boys to her, she drove them back to the cabin in Old Jimmy, poste-haste.

"Red alert, boys," she said, rushing them into the cabin, willing the panic from her voice. "Remember what that means?"

Nodding gravely, Teddy took Charlie's hand and they disappeared into the loft to gather their backpacks as Sarah woke Ethan. He'd been up most of the night filling in the blanks in Bibi's story and Sarah had sent him off to bed that morning after finding him half-asleep over the laptop.

"What's up, sweetheart?" Ethan said around a jaw-popping yawn.

"There's a blue Ford Focus," Sarah, her heart galloping in her chest. "Oh, blast it. I was supposed to remember the license number, wasn't I? I'm sorry."

Ethan kissed her. "Not important. Where are Teddy and Charlie?"

Filling her lungs with a shuddering breath, Sarah replied, "Waiting for me."

"Go to the cave and wait for me," he said and she spun away.

First donning his grandfather's hunting vest which was already loaded with ammunition, bear spray and anything else Sarah had been able to fit in the many pockets, Ethan then grabbed his Glock, tucking it in the back of his jeans. Skirting the thick evergreens lining the drive, Ethan soon spotted the Focus and, to his surprise, recognized his father in the driver's seat. *What is he doing here?*

As soon as Ethan stepped out of cover, Robert pulled alongside and lowered his window.

"I've come to warn you," he said. "They're very close, son. Both Stevie and Ryan have been questioned in regards to your disappearance. The Bureau has already searched my house twice."

"Were you followed?" Ethan asked with all humor erased from his mind.

Robert frowned. "Me? Really, son, I'm a better cop than that. I assume that no one has found your connection to this cabin."

"I had to shoot a grizzly but I wasn't able to kill it," Ethan said, still angry at his failure to complete the necessary task.

His father immediately understood the implications. "Then they won't be far behind. Do you have a plan for the beautiful Sarah and her two little sons?"

"You, Dad," Ethan replied, his response masked by the whirr of chopper thrumming over the horizon. His heart twisting in his chest, Ethan grasped his father's arm. "Teddy and Charlie. You have to take them Dad. They're in my cave where I used to hide when I was a kid. Do you know it?"

"I always knew where it was but where do I take them, son?" Robert asked urgently.

"Take them to Sarah's father," Ethan said. "Everything you need is in Teddy's pack."

"Does Sarah know where to go?" Robert asked.

Nodding, Ethan said, "She calls Johnny Parsons and then meets him at the nearest police station."

Robert nodded. "Go."

Trusting his father to do his job, Ethan ran full-tilt to the cabin, prepared to do his. Coming to the front edge of the cabin, he glanced around the corner and his heart fell with an avalanche of fear into his belly, the image forever imprinted on his mind: his darling Sarah kneeling, her hands linked behind her head, staring down the barrel of a shotgun.

CHAPTER 19

Robert Lange crept through the bush, slowly and soundlessly making his way through the labyrinth to his middle son's haven of retreat. Quickly and quietly, he pulled the bushes back across the opening to camouflage the cave's entrance.

"Teddy," he whispered. "Charlie. It's Papa Bert. Come out very quietly."

Teddy poked his head out from behind a large rock. "Papa Bert? There was a big noise."

"I know, son. You were very brave to stay hidden. Is Charlie with you?" Robert said.

Charlie poked up from behind Teddy. "Papa Bert!"

"Shhh!" Robert reminded him. Opening wide his arms, he said, "Come here, my boys." The little boys crossed the distance quickly and threw themselves into his arms.

"Where's mommy?" Teddy asked.

"She's with Ethan," Robert said. "They have a few things to do to make it safe for you two. She will find you as soon as she can. I promise."

"What do we do, Papa?" Teddy said with real fear in his voice.

"You can stay with me. I'll keep you safe, boys. Will that be okay?" Robert said.

"Want Mama an' Eefan," Charlie whined, beginning to cry.

"There, there boys. I'll protect you," Robert said, holding them close. "Let's stay here a bit longer and then we'll find a safe place to wait for Mommy and Ethan. I'll take you to your Grandpa's house. Okay?"

Teddy tried to console his little brother. "Okay, Papa, okay. It's okay, Charlie. Ethan will find us. He's scary sometimes but he always finds us. Right, Charlie?"

Charlie nodded seriously and his tears began to dry up. "Mama."

"Yep," Teddy replied, seeming to understand exactly what his brother meant. "Mommy will find us, too." Teddy patted his brother's back kindly and then turned his face back into Robert's chest.

"Mommy will find you," Robert promised, keeping the boys on his lap long after the helicopter departed and the trucks drove away.

Ethan drove, keeping to the speed limit, checking his mirrors and generally obeying the rules of the road. He surveyed the landscape out of habit rather than necessity. One Explorer drove ahead of them and two behind. The helicopter hovered above.

Before he'd even be able to formulate a strategy for rescuing Sarah, Ethan had found himself face down on the ground beside her. McCreary with Bella Farini at his elbow had taken one disgusted look at them and then ordered them into a black Ford Explorer.

Ethan was ordered to drive. Ethan cooperated, knowing that, for the moment, he had no chance of escape that wouldn't lead to Sarah's harm. He couldn't allow that. He needed to keep her alive more than he needed to escape, and for the moment, here was the safest place, drawing the bad guys further and further from Teddy and Charlie.

"Ethan?" Sarah whispered. She was utterly pale, sitting beside him stiffly and wringing her hands in her lap. "What about them?"

Ethan knew that she was asking about Teddy and Charlie and he realized that she was less terrified than he'd previously thought. She was furious because he'd broken his promise to save the boys. But how could he reassure her without giving them away?

"Trust me," was all he could say.

She seemed to process that information, or lack thereof, for a time, and then finished with a small shake of her head.

A clue. Ethan needed to offer her hope. "Bert," he said.

Her brows narrowed in confusion and then rose in hope. Leaning forward, she studied his face and he felt like he could feel her dismay in the intensity of her stare.

"Really?" she whispered in a voice that was barely there. Ethan nodded once. Her relief was palpable and Ethan worried that their backseat companions might pick up on the change in emotion. But he needn't have worried. They were thickheads.

"Ethan?" Sarah said in a conversational tone. Ethan turned to glimpse a conniving expression on her face that rapidly disappeared.

Reaching over, Ethan took her hand, needing some contact. "What is it, sweetheart?"

"I need to use the washroom," Sarah said and Ethan knew her plan. She didn't trust him. She was going to run and find her children. Perhaps that would be best. McCreary wanted him so maybe he would let Sarah get away.

"Hands back on the wheel!" Jenkins, the beefy guy with severe halitosis, demanded, nudging Ethan in the back of the head with the shotgun. Clenching his jaw, he brought Sarah's hand up to rest against the wheel, still firmly clasped in his. Jenkins was not amused. "Release her hand and replace your own on the steering wheel," he said, expressing his foul breath into Ethan's face.

Ethan kissed the back of her hand and released it, saying, "She needs to stop."

"Later," Hopper insisted, the short, skinny guy with the face of a ferret.

"You ever traveled with a woman, Hopper?" Ethan said. "You stop when they need to stop or face the consequences."

Ethan heard a strange whirring sound followed by a click. He glanced over to see Hopper obsessively spinning the cylinder of his Smith & Wesson Model 10. Three whirr-clicks and then Hopper pulled out his cell phone and called in, requesting permission to stop. "Fine," he said sharply to Ethan, another whirr and a click accompanying his words. "Pull over to the side of the road."

"At least let me find her a tree." Annoyed, Ethan persisted.

"To hide behind?" Hopper said, scoffing. "I don't think so."

"Look, you've got Bella with you. She can escort her, right?" Ethan said, still trying to find a way to get Sarah away and back to Teddy and Charlie. Sarah was right not to trust him. He certainly hadn't done a very good job keeping her and the children safe up to this point, what with bombs and bears.

Hopper dialed his cell again, having a stilted conversation full of "yes" and "no" and little else.

"Pull over there," Hopper instructed him, pointing with his handgun. "Stay in the car." Whirr-click. "Hands on the wheel, Lange."

Ethan watched as Bella stepped out of the lead Explorer, coming to open Sarah's door. Why did the FBI insist on buying only black SUVs?

"Go ahead, Sarah," Ethan said to her, sending a message of more than the words spoken. Surprising him, she leaned back to kiss him. In that moment, he wanted so badly to hold her against him for all time, to close his eyes and be once again in her arms with Teddy and Charlie playing around them. He wanted to be her husband, to be Teddy and Charlie's daddy and live the rest of his life as a family. But desire didn't make it so.

Walking side by side with Bella to the crowd of bushes in the middle of the field beside the road, Sarah could feel Ethan's eyes tracing her every step. He had told her to go, to make a run for it. She knew that's what he was telling her, hoping in Bella's loyalty despite the evidence to the contrary.

"Bella, what's going on?" Sarah asked.

"I know how this looks Sarah," Bella said. "But some books have counterfeit covers."

"But which is the counterfeit, today or yesterday?" Sarah mumbled.

"McCreary is the real deal. He has no connection to our wannabe congresswoman. You're safest here," Bella said.

"Are they going to hurt Ethan?" Sarah said.

"This isn't Burma, Sarah. We have laws here," Bella said.

"Your laws have changed somewhat of late, I'm well aware," Sarah muttered.

"Not that much," Bella replied. She didn't sound annoyed, but rather mournful.

"Ethan wants me to run," Sarah said, pausing before she slipped behind the bushes.

"If you run, Vakh will find you and kill you," Bella said deliberately. "McCreary is your last, best chance."

Oh, Father, show me what to do. Finishing her business behind the bushes, Sarah waited for a booming voice from the heavens but heard only the still, small voice which told her to stay with Ethan. *Okay, Father. I trust you.*

As Sarah rose and adjusted her clothing, Bella stepped forward, pressing a solid, cylindrical object into her hand. Sarah slipped it into her pocket without checking to see what it was. The two women returned to the vehicles together.

Smiling to reassure Ethan, Sarah rested her hand on his leg. Narrowing his eyes at her, he nonverbally asked the question, *why didn't you run?* She squeezed his thigh, trying to reassure him and remove the sorrow from his gaze.

Turning, Sarah fixed Jenkins with a stern glare. "Where are we going?" she said.

"Denver. There's a field office there," Ethan replied.

Slapping Ethan across the back of the head, Jenkins commanded, "Shut up and drive."

Sarah watched the muscles bunch in Ethan's jaw, loving that he tolerated the situation to keep her and Teddy and

Charlie safe. She was furious, however, with the two thickheads in the back seat. Subsiding into silence, she rested her head against the seat and watched the Colorado countryside pass her by.

Ethan saw the helicopter. Again. It wasn't the black helicopter which had delivered McCreary and his agents and then followed them to the Colorado border. It was gray and, because his training had prepared his brain to automatically log away the registration numbers on the chopper's tail, he knew that it was the same helicopter that had followed them for a time two days out of Little Rock.

"Sarah," he whispered, nodding at the sky when she looked over at him. Scanning the skies, he could tell the moment she spotted it because she stiffened and her eyes widened in recognition.

"You don't think—" she began.

"Quiet!" Jenkins demanded, shoving the back of her seat.

"You see that Bell up there?" Ethan pointed at the approaching helicopter.

"Bell? What are you talking about? Shut up!" Hopper said. The rate of the whirr-click of his Smith & Wesson seemed to increase with Hopper's level of agitation.

"Bell helicopter," Ethan exaggerated his articulation.

Jenkins narrowed his eyes, calling in on his cell phone. "Probably belongs to the local fire department."

"Local? Are you sure?" Ethan said dubiously.

Jenkins phoned in again. "Not local. Oklahoma."

"We spotted the same chopper on our way to Colorado," Ethan informed him.

"So what?" Hopper snapped at him.

But Ethan could tell that he was now interested. "It's not unusual for ex-Marines to get jobs in the Fire Department, is it?"

"Marines?" Jenkins asked, clearly confused.

"One of the attacks on a safe house was led by an ex-Marine," Ethan said.

Jenkins dialed again, speaking furiously. Soon Ethan was ordered to pull over to the side of the road. Jerked out of the vehicle, Ethan was zip cuffed and forced to his knees. Fortunately, no one seemed to care that Ethan had left the driver side window open and Sarah could hear everything.

McCreary approached looking very irritated. "Now, what's this all about?" he said.

Ethan quickly responded, "I've seen that helicopter before. Two days out of Little Rock."

"And your point?" McCreary said. With his hands tucked behind his back, his navy blue sweater vest neatly covering his freshly starched pale blue shirt, he looked implacable. Only the slight elevation of one eyebrow gave away any interest at all.

Ethan narrowed his eyes in irritation. "Are you willing to listen?"

"I'm standing here when I could be drinking my coffee," McCreary replied languidly as though that explained everything.

"Senator Tom Baker's wife is connected to the Chechen mercenary Borz Vakh. She is also connected to the Marines through her husband and a rumored affair. One of the attacks on the safe house where Sarah and I were kept was perpetrated by an ex-Marine, Rico Soldat. It is not unusual for ex-Marines to join the fire department," Ethan said. "Look up. That helicopter is getting closer."

Holding out one hand, McCreary snapped his fingers. "Bring me binoculars." McCreary studied the approaching chopper diligently for several minutes adjusting the focus several times. Suddenly his hands clenched on the eye pieces. "Get him inside the vehicle," he said. "Go!"

Slicing the plastic of the zip cuffs hastily, Ethan was quickly freed by Jenkins, not even noticing the slice left behind on the palm of his hand. Everyone scattered to their vehicles. Just as they roared onto the highway, bullets scored the asphalt in a path directly at the car containing Ethan and Sarah.

Swerving, Ethan accelerated, roaring around the Explorer in front of him and out into the lead. No one was smacking him in the head now for excessive speeding and independent thought. They were urging him on.

"How do they know which car I'm in?" Ethan demanded to know but no one had an answer for him.

Turning a hard left, Ethan raced off the highway onto a maze of smaller roads, heading toward a complex of mills he'd spotted from the highway. He hoped to lose the chopper amidst the buildings. The other cars followed. There was no point in trying to create a diversion to distract the chopper pilot. The helicopter's shifting trajectory made it obvious that the pilot's only interest was in Ethan's SUV.

Speeding along the bumpy road, Ethan swerved to keep the car out of the direct line of bullets which kept lancing toward them. On the next pass, the helicopter paused in front of them.

"Sarah, get down!" Ethan said, pushing her down on the seat. Bullets shattered the windshield, punching into the seat beside him, directly above her head.

Without hesitation, Ethan drove into the field beside him, turning a wide arc to reach the warehouses, working to keep the helicopter from getting in front of them again. Soon he heard the return of gunfire from the vehicles surrounding them. Accelerating, ignoring the spin of the rear wheels, Ethan finally gained the cover of the buildings, speeding directly toward the large bay doors directly ahead.

"Sarah, brace yourself!" he cried.

The incredible force of their crash smashed them through the doors of the building and safely inside, the air bags deploying. The world went black.

"Ethan! Please wake up!"

Ethan gradually became aware that he was lying on his back. He could smell grain and baby powder…and lavender. Someone was pulling at his shirt and his head drummed a rhythm of pain and he wanted his mother. *No wait. My mother is dead.* Then who wanted so desperately to wake him? *Sarah!*

"Sarah?" he groaned.

"Oh, Ethan," Sarah cried against him, burying her face in his shirt. His arms felt leaden but he wanted to hold her and he wanted to know what was going on. Last thing he remembered was driving to Denver. Then a helicopter…what?

"Sarah? What happened?" he asked, finishing his words with a cough as the dust in the air seemed to catch in his dry throat.

"You saved us, sweetheart. They fired on us. Bella was shot and a couple of other officers were injured in their vehicles. You drove us into this grain warehouse and saved us," Sarah said.

"You okay?" he asked weakly.

"I'm fine. But you've been out for half an hour. Can you move?" she said.

"Don't know," Ethan said. He concentrated on his toes. Yep, they moved and then his legs. Yep. His left hand moved but his right? He finally opened his eyes and looked down. Sarah followed his gaze and moved back quickly. She'd been kneeling by his hand, trapping it against his side. He had an urge to giggle. *Have I ever giggled in my life?* Lifting his hand, he brushed a few strands of grain from her hair. Grabbing hold, she clasped his hand against her face, kissing the palm.

"Are you okay?" she asked, deep concern in her voice.

"I think so. All my parts ache and my head hurts like the dickens but—" Pushing up on his elbows, he said, "Yep, I'm fully functioning."

She pulled him into her arms and sobbed against him. "I love you. Don't ever scare me like that again."

"Just don't hit me okay? I don't think there's a single unbruised inch on my body," Ethan said.

"Okay, baby," she said and he smiled, pulling her onto his lap, enjoying the sensation of being close.

Eventually McCreary came over to them. Rather than the sneer he usually wore his wide eyes revealed shock and the first hints of suspicion. He began speaking and then had to clear his throat to continue. "Well, Mr. Lange, it seems that you were telling the truth about our Chechen friend. There is a conspiracy and someone really is out to get you."

A sigh of relief burst from Ethan's lungs. "Yes, sir. Did you catch him?" he asked optimistically.

McCreary shook his head. "One of my officers managed to down the helicopter. Two of the men were killed..." He paused. "Including Vakh."

"Are you sure it was Vakh?" Ethan demanded to know, his hopes of interrogating the mercenary fading quickly.

"Yes. I identified him myself," McCreary admitted.

"What about the third man?" Ethan said.

"The pilot?" McCreary said. "He doesn't seem to know anything. Just doing a favor for a friend."

"Argh!" Ethan growled.

"Mr. McCreary," Sarah began, encouraged to continue when McCreary met her gaze. "If you've caught the terrorist, is Ethan finally free to go? Am I free to go?"

"I'm sorry, Mrs. Maier, but Mr. Lange still has charges to answer. As for you, we will need your testimony. But I don't see why you should be inconvenienced for long." McCreary started to walk away and then turned back. "We leave in fifteen minutes."

Drawing Sarah close, Ethan held her tightly until it was time to go. This time, an officer drove the vehicle and Ethan and Sarah were left together in the back seat.

Not realizing she'd slept, Sarah was awakened when her pillow, which had been Ethan's leg, slipped from beneath her head. Glancing aside in panic, she saw Ethan led out of the car and forced to kneel on the pavement while they trapped his wrists in zip cuffs again. Tears moistened her eyes as she followed behind, walking where she was led.

Signing in the prisoners, McCreary ordered them taken to a holding cell and monitored. A guard returned for Ethan but brought him back again a half hour or so later wearing a gray coverall in place of his clothes.

"What did they do?" Sarah asked.

"Strip search," Ethan grumbled.

"Oh."

Ethan smirked at her. "Was that a leer I just witnessed in your eyes?"

Blushing deeply, she denied it and then relented to honesty. "Perhaps, just curiosity. Now, stop teasing me." Embarrassed and confused and frightened, Sarah moved over to the only bed in the room, a single metal frame topped with a lumpy, stained mattress. Sarah sat with her back against the wall, her knees drawn up to her chest as Ethan paced the room.

"I'm frightened," she said, hoping to gain his attention. He stopped and she watched him put aside his own worries to comfort her.

"It'll be okay, honey," he said.

She turned her face into his chest. "Do you think Teddy and Charlie are safe?"

Ethan reached a hand up to lightly stroke her cheek running his thumb across her chin. "Dad will guard them with his life. Do you know what he said to me?" He paused, waiting for her to meet his gaze. "He said they were his first grandsons."

Her eyes widened. "But they're not—we're not—"

Tipping her chin with his thumb and index finger, he asked, "Could we fix that, Sarah? When this is over and the four of us are together again, would you...do you think you'd want to...will you marry me?"

She watched him closely for a moment and then burst into laughter. "You have appalling timing! But if you come to us when this is all over and ask me properly then, yes, I will marry you, for Teddy and Charlie because I think you'll be a wonderful father. And for me, because I love you."

Ethan pulled her close along his body holding her tightly to him. "Do you know what we've never done?" he said.

"What?" she said.

"I have never taken you dancing," he said, pulling her up from the mattress and into his arms as he began twirling her around the dirty concrete floor of the holding cell, their bare feet slapping softly. Ethan hummed in her ear.

"Are you humming and dancing to Amazing Grace?" she teased.

"It's the first song that came into my mind," he admitted as they continued dancing, drawing comfort from each other. "Sarah?" She hmmm'ed against his chest. "When they come to offer you your phone call, I think you should call Johnny." He moved closer to whisper in her ear. "He has a plan all ready to begin."

She nodded. "What are you going to do when they come for you?"

"I'm going to tell them everything," he replied calmly.

She looked up in surprise. "Really? Why? Do you trust them? Bella said that McCreary was our last, best chance. Is it true?"

"I don't know about that but I do know a few things. These guys know that I'm in love with you and so the first thing they'll do is threaten you to get me to talk. I won't let you be harmed in any way. Secondly, McCreary is reputed to be a hard, arrogant blaggard but ruthlessly honest. Thirdly, there are no Marines in the outfit that captured us. These are honest to goodness Feds. I no longer care about my career, sweetheart, I only care about getting to a resolution, to a situation, a place, where I can be with you and Teddy and Charlie like a proper family."

They subsided into silence for a time, just enjoying being together without much anxiety because there wasn't really anything they could do at the moment except pray and that was something they could do together.

"Ahem," McCreary interrupted their dance. "Mrs. Maier, I've come to offer you your phone call."

"Thank you," she responded, tiptoeing up to kiss Ethan before she moved to follow McCreary to the telephone.

"By the way," McCreary said in a conversational tone. "I just received word that your children have landed safely at Pearson International Airport in Toronto with a Robert Lange. They were going to stop Mr. Lange until they double-checked the first name and let him pass. Apparently, a Thaddeus David Maier and Charles Henry Maier were reunited with their grandfather."

"They're safe?" Sarah asked meekly, tears of relief springing to her eyes.

"They are quite safe," McCreary confirmed kindly then narrowed his eyes as though to study her response.

"Thank you," she whispered.

Sarah called Johnny just as Ethan had suggested. He promised to be there ASAP and he promised to contact her father before departing to tell Teddy and Charlie that Mommy would be home soon.

The lawyer arrived about an hour before Johnny did and then it was time to leave.

"Come for me," Sarah said to Ethan, weeping openly in his arms.

"I will always come for you, my love," Ethan promised.

And then she was led away to rejoin her children and he was led away to interrogation.

CHAPTER 20

T ying the half-Windsor on his navy and red striped tie, Ethan prepared for his last day in the FBI. The enquiry had resumed as soon as Sarah left and it had been grueling. They'd mercilessly dismantled Ethan's entire career first with the FBI and then with the FBI's special clandestine operation, the CAUDO Project, but in the end had concluded that he was not criminally culpable in the death of Senator Tom Baker. However, because he'd neglected to fulfill his duties as expected as an officer by fleeing prosecution across state lines, and jeopardized the lives of three civilians by not submitting them for protection, he was formally reprimanded. And because there was no concrete evidence to link Bibi Baker to Borz Vakh, the death of Senator Tom Baker was still considered Ethan's responsibility. With only circumstantial evidence linking Bibi and Vakh, and even with McCreary's testimony that it was indeed Vakh who had targeted Ethan, Ethan couldn't be released of responsibility. It was impossible to prove whether the senator had been killed before or after Ethan had confronted Vakh. As a result, Ethan's employment with the Federal Bureau of Investigation had been terminated with two weeks' notice. He'd been released with no references and a huge black stain on his record.

For the last two weeks of his career, he'd been assigned to duty as a desk officer. Today was his last day processing fitness reports on field agents. At the end of the day, he'd turn in his badge and his gun and…what? Tomorrow, he'd no longer be a federal agent and would likely never be allowed to work in any form of law enforcement again. How could he go to Sarah like this, with nothing to offer except unemployment and poverty? It had taken his last penny to pay for the lawyer who had represented him and Sarah.

Ethan's morose thoughts were interrupted by the doorbell. Making his way to the front door, he gulped down the rest of his cold coffee from the pot he'd made at three o'clock this morning. He hadn't been sleeping or eating properly, missing Sarah and the kids grievously.

Opening the door, he was shocked to see—

"Johnny?"

Johnny Parsons stepped past him into his house, grinning broadly. "Ethan, man, where have you been? You know that our Sarah is waiting for you, don't you?"

"Come in," Ethan mumbled after the fact, gesturing to the man who ironically already stood within his house. "Do you want some coffee?"

"Yes. Definitely. Show me where and I'll teach you a little trick I learned during the night shift back when Dave and I were with CSIS."

Ethan showed Johnny to his kitchen and stood back to watch him empty and reload the coffee maker, adding a pinch of cinnamon and a drop of vanilla to the grounds.

Grimacing, Ethan watched in disbelief. "What are you doing?"

"Trust me," Johnny replied, still grinning.

Not cheered by the man's ebullience, Ethan came to lean against the counter beside Sarah's husband's friend. "How is Sarah?" Ethan asked quietly. "And the boys?"

"They are safe. They are healthy, but my girl is not happy, man," Johnny said, filling the carafe.

Subconsciously, Ethan clenched his teeth when Johnny referred to her that way. *Sarah is my girl. But what do I have to offer her?* His angst subsided into sorrow again. "What's wrong?" he asked.

"She misses you, wonders when you're coming. Said you promised you'd come," Johnny said.

Ethan turned away. "I've been fired, Johnny, deemed unreliable and unfit for service. I have no money, no job. How can I go to her when I have nothing to offer?"

"Offer her yourself," Johnny said as though the matter was simple and Ethan was a simpleton for not seeing it.

Ethan snorted. "Myself! And what about Teddy and Charlie? They need a father, not some—I don't know—me. I don't know if I can be a good father to them. If I mess it up with them, Sarah will hate me."

"She knows you're not perfect, Ethan. Do you think David was perfect?" Johnny snorted this time. "He had his own fair share of quirks and idiosyncrasies. She wants you, Ethan. Don't you dare disappoint her!" Ethan watched Johnny dubiously, not missing the flash in the man's eyes. Suddenly snapping his fingers, Johnny changed the subject, "Oh, yes. That reminds me." He produced a small, cylindrical object from his pocket, holding it out where Ethan could see it. "Sarah ordered me to give this to you. Evidently someone called Bella gave it to her."

Ethan took it from Johnny, turning it slowly in his hands. "A memory stick?"

"Yup! Want to see what's on it?" Johnny said, rubbing his palms conspiratorially.

Ethan's shrug lacked enthusiasm. "Sure," he said, leading the way to his laptop which had been removed from his ransacked house and eventually returned to him completely erased. He plugged the memory stick into the USB port and waited. It whirred and loaded. Soon the menu produced a list of documents: Eleanor "Bibi" Baker; Known Terrorists – Borz Vakh; Counter-surveillance including links to Jack Dietrich; and Sarah.

In spite of all that had happened and the deep desire Ethan had to prove his innocence in the death of Tom Baker, his first instinct was to read the message from Sarah. He resisted the urge, however, opening the other files first. There before him scrolled page after page of the information he'd been seeking, the final proof of his theory that Bibi Baker had arranged with a mercenary to eliminate her husband and frame Ethan Lange for the crime. The lines of data included testimony by a cleaner that Tom Baker had been killed before the FBI arrived on the scene.

Ethan's heart beat a tattoo as he read the last collection of documents, the intelligence collected that Jack Dietrich was a mole. He had been in league with Bibi and the Chechen all along, feeding them information on Ethan's movements and plans. Ethan was angry with himself for not having guessed. Once in the past he had believed that Dietrich was crooked and he'd been correct. Relieved and furious in equal measures, Ethan stood and walked away from the computer, running his hands through his hair, trying to process the betrayal.

"Has Sarah seen this?" Ethan asked, gesturing behind him to the computer.

"No. She wrote you a letter there…" Johnny pointed at the file tag on the screen. "But asked me to look through the documents and see if they could help you. Once I confirmed that they would indeed be very useful to you, she sent me down here to deliver it. She seems to think I'm your personal assistant these days."

Ignoring the man's wry attempt at humor, Ethan returned to the laptop. "Johnny," Ethan said, looking up into the man's eyes. "Do you think I could have a moment alone?"

"Sure, man. I'll go have my coffee on the back porch. It's a beautiful day in Washington," Johnny announced moving out into the sunshine.

"Thanks," Ethan murmured, not seeing sunshine anywhere in his life. Waiting until Johnny moved away, he opened the letter from Sarah.

Dear Ethan,

I'm not sure why you've stayed away. Johnny says you've been cleared of all charges, that they are just going to fire you. Isn't that what we wanted?

The boys miss you terribly. I'm very disappointed that you changed your mind about us but I wanted you to know that Teddy and Charlie love you. Thank you for all you did to protect us. I remember now that you wouldn't promise not to break my heart so I'll try to forgive you for hurting me.

Please be safe and well and at least call the boys. They miss you.

Ethan's heart dropped like a stone within him. She'd given up on him. She thought he didn't love her.

"I forgot to give you this." Johnny appeared suddenly at Ethan's shoulder, holding out a white envelope. "It's also from Sarah."

Quickly brushing his hands across his face to erase the evidence of his deep sorrow, Ethan took the envelope in his shaking hands. Inside he found a piece of lined paper clearly hastily torn from a notebook and covered in blue marker scrawl.

Dear Ethan,

I can't let Johnny leave without writing this as well. Ignore my other letter. I love you. It's true that Teddy and Charlie love you, too,

but I forgot to tell you that I love you and miss you and I want you to come for us just as you said you would. Come for us so we can be a real family. I don't care what you do for a living or where we have to live though I think I'd enjoy living in your grandfather's cabin as long as you stay away from rattlesnakes—oh, yes, and I promise to stay away from grizzly bears.

Ethan, please come home. We love you.

Yours Always, Sarah

"Thank you," Ethan said to Johnny, his future suddenly crystal clear. "There's just one more thing I need to do."

"It's your life, man, but are you sure you want to wait?" Johnny watched him dubiously.

Ethan nodded confidently, assured in his decision. "Yes. If I deal with this, then I can be truly free."

"It's her birthday on Friday. She and the boys are celebrating at her father's house. Will you be there?" Johnny said

"I don't know," Ethan admitted.

Johnny frowned. "What do you want me to tell her?"

"Tell her not to lose faith in me. Tell her...tell her...tell her I love her." Ethan looked into Johnny's face expecting derision but he saw only admiration. The men shook hands firmly and Johnny departed.

His heart lightened within him, Ethan returned to his desk, picking up the telephone. "Agent McCreary? This is Ethan Lange. I have something that I think you should see."

Sarah scoured the news in every format for information regarding rogue FBI agents, Chechen mercenaries and senator's wives. She cheered when Bibi Baker's bid for senate was withdrawn. She rejoiced when Borz Vakh was finally reported as the villain behind the attempted assassination of an unknown FBI agent. When the news broke that Vakh was linked to Baker in the assassination of her husband, Sarah wanted to have a party, but there was still no news from Ethan. Days passed into weeks and weeks into a month and more and still she had no word from him. The boys still asked daily when Ethan was coming. In spite of his absence, though, they'd settled into a happy routine that Sarah promoted but didn't share.

Sarah had decided to celebrate her birthday at her father's house, hoping that being surrounded by familiarity would take some of the sting out of marking the day without any assurance about her future. But she was feeling terribly alone within the crowd of family and friends.

"Sarah, my girl, what are we going to do with you?" Johnny asked in mock despair, wrapping her in a bear hug.

"Where is he, Johnny?" Sarah said, pushing out of his hug to meet his gaze. "He said he would come for us. Have you heard anything more? They didn't send him to prison, did they?"

"No, Sarah," Johnny said, exasperated. "He's not going to prison. You know that. I told you that before. He's no longer facing any charges, in fact. That evidence you sent with me was very important and he's just using it to tie up some loose ends. Jack Dietrich turned out to be part of the conspiracy."

"His team leader?" Sarah exclaimed. "What about the others? Bella and Owen?"

"Don't know. He mentioned a Brigitte," Johnny said.

A pang of jealousy hit Sarah square between the eyes. "Brigitte. Maybe that's where he's gone," she muttered darkly.

Johnny responded with a loud guffaw. "Sarah, you are too easy to bait. He has not gone to Brigitte or Bella or Marilyn Monroe."

Johnny's laugh forced a momentary smile from Sarah. "Oh, what have they done to him to prevent him from coming?" she asked, exasperated.

"They've reprimanded him for escaping custody and not informing the bureau of the threat to your life but with the evidence of a connection between the senator's wife and the terrorist, they've allowed him to resign rather than firing him. I hear he has several job offers already, MI-5, CSIS, Interpol, even the NSA has tried to recruit him," Johnny said.

Sarah's shoulders slumped even further. "Maybe he's decided to move on without us."

"What did you get for your birthday?" Johnny asked with a cheerful voice, clearly trying to change the subject.

"Hmmm? Oh, a new watch, a blender and a few books. Now that you mention it where's your present? Didn't forget to get me one, did you?" A tiny playful smile pulled at the corner of her mouth but it never touched her heart.

"It's on its way, I promise," Johnny said as the doorbell rang.

"Can you get that, please?" Sarah asked. "I'm just not up to pretending to be happy."

"As you wish," Johnny said, bowing out of the room. Sarah turned back to the window, watching the little family of ducks on the pond.

"So who was it?" she asked Johnny when he returned.

"Me. Happy Birthday, my girl." But the voice wasn't Johnny's it was Ethan's, husky and warm and thrilling.

Sarah spun to see him, standing before her looking worn and weathered and utterly handsome, studying her carefully and awaiting her response. Flying into his arms, she clasped him tightly to her, feeling his strong arms return the embrace. Breathing deeply, she inhaled the familiar spicy scent of him.

In the midst of joy, a sudden anger rose up within her and Sarah shoved him in the chest. "What took you so long?"

Ethan pulled her tighter against him. "I lost everything, Sarah," he said quietly. "I couldn't come to you with nothing. And then you sent the information that saved me and I wanted to wait until everything was settled so I could come to you free and ready to start a new life."

Calming slightly and resting her head against his shoulder, she said, "You...you could have let me know you were safe." She wasn't quite ready to let him off the hook yet.

"I knew that once I heard your voice I'd be lost and wouldn't be able to stay away," he said. "I asked Johnny to watch over you. And encourage you not to lose hope in me." Pulling back, he met her gaze, brushing her hair back from her face. "Did you lose hope in me?"

"Hope is all I've lived on for the past weeks. Why did you wait so long?" she said.

"Honestly?" he asked, his thumbs stroking her cheeks tenderly.

"Always," she confirmed.

"I couldn't believe that you would really want me now. I was fired, my future taken from me. I was afraid that if I came and made a hash of things with your children, you would grow to hate me. I couldn't stand the thought of that," he said.

"But now you know better?" she asked, looking up into his deep blue eyes.

"Yes. Without Dietrich's vengeance and Bibi and Vakh's conspiracy, I never would have met you, Sarah, and I never would have found God again. I love you, Sarah. I would tread through danger and fire and rattlesnakes and grizzly bears again a hundred times to be at your side," he said with power and determination in his eyes.

"Are you really here for good? Is it over?"

"Done and dusted," he said emphatically, kissing her loudly on the cheek. "I was going to come to you with a new job too but then I realized that my decision was really yours as well."

"What do you mean?" she asked, wondering how many different emotions she could experience in a single hour.

He was still holding her close as he gently stroked his palm up and down her back. "It's not just about me and my career anymore. The job I take determines where I live, where we live. I want to do what's best for Teddy and Charlie. I want to make you happy. I want the four of us to be a family, to own a house in a good neighborhood, near a good school and a good church. I no longer see myself as my job. With you a part of it, there is so much more to my life than my job."

Draping her arms around his neck, she asked, "What do you see in yourself, what have you learned?"

"I'm no longer willing to forfeit the happiness of those I love for anything. I won't bury my feelings deeper than my heart ever again," he said.

With her face tipped to him, she could see the moment when he could no longer resist the urge to kiss her long and deep, reminding her of the very essence of him. And that's how Johnny found them, locked in an embrace, transported away from anything but the sensation of love.

Johnny cleared his throat. "There are two little boys out here who would like to give their mother her birthday cake."

He was three words in before Sarah became aware that anyone existed beyond Ethan. Her cheeks flushed, her heart warm, she pulled back to see Ethan in the same state and laughed with joy as she imagined the picture they must present.

"Thanks, Johnny." She stepped over to give him a peck on the cheek. "I really, really like my birthday present."

Johnny chuckled and shook Ethan's hand firmly. "You take care of our Sarah now, you hear?"

"I do indeed and I intend to," Ethan replied, returning Johnny's friendly grin.

"Ethan?" Sarah extended her hand to him and he moved over to take hers.

"Yes?" he breathed.

"Let's go see our family." Holding Ethan's hand firmly in her own, Sarah rejoined the party ongoing in the living room.

"Eefan! You comed home!" Charlie cried in greeting, running and leaping into the man's arms. "Come see G'mpa." Charlie wiggled down and led Ethan by the hand to a man in his late sixties, balding and strongly built; no one to be trifled with. Charlie kept one hand in Ethan's and slapped the older man on the back where he crouched before one of his grandchildren. Pushing off his knees and turning to stand before Ethan, his movements revealed that the grandchild he'd been speaking with was Teddy who had been showing off his newest dinosaur and receiving a mini-lecture on the habitats of herbivores.

Teddy's eyes widened in astonishment and his jaw dropped open.

"Hello Teddy," Ethan said and Sarah could see that he was clearly uncertain of the boy's response.

"I missed you," Teddy replied quietly.

"I missed you, too, very much," Ethan said.

That was what Teddy needed to hear. He bounded into Ethan's arms, hugging him tightly around the neck as Ethan kissed him on the cheek. Charlie tried to crawl up Ethan's leg to get in on the hug. Dropping to his knees, Ethan wrapped them both in his arms until they released him.

"This is my Grandpa Johnson," Teddy said by way of introduction and then led Ethan over to a second man of commensurate age, this one with iron gray hair, tall and slender, standing beside a plump and happy woman who exuded joy in her every movement. "This is my Grandpa Maier and my Grandma Maier."

Suddenly self-conscious, Ethan's belly fluttered with insecurity at the prospect of meeting the parents of his rival...even though he knew the feeling was ridiculous. And yet, how would they feel about the man who sought to take their son's place in their grandchildren's lives? He needn't have worried. Mrs. Maier took him by the shoulders and kissed him on both cheeks, happily welcoming him to the birthday party. Mr. Maier merely nodded and shook Ethan's hand. Teddy tugged on Ethan's other hand and he bent down to listen to what the boy had to say.

"He never smiles but he's really nice." Ethan grinned at Teddy's soft-spoken words and then waited as the boy fidgeted and stuttered through his next question. "Ethan, are you going away again?"

"Well, I have one more question to ask before I know for certain," Ethan replied, winking at Teddy.

Taking Teddy and Charlie by the hands, Ethan led them over to Sarah who had watched the entire interchange with a smile on her face, a smile that brightened her eyes and made them sparkle. Releasing the boys' hands, Ethan took Sarah's and knelt on one knee before her in the room filled with her family and friends.

"Meeting you and your sons has been the greatest experience of my life. I want to be with you and Teddy and Charlie. I want to be their daddy and I want to be your husband, Sarah. I love you," Ethan said. "I love you more than cats love catnip, more than bears love honey, more than Stevie likes to eat beetles." She laughed in utter joy at his words. "I promise to love you all, to honor you and to protect you whatever comes. Sarah, will you marry me?" As he asked the question, he pulled a blue velvet box from his pocket, holding it out to her.

Overjoyed in the moment, Sarah beamed a brilliant smile as she responded to his earnest proposal, "Yes. On behalf of Teddy and Charlie and me, I accept."

Slipping the sapphire and diamond ring onto her finger, Ethan rose and wrapped her in a hug, kissing her briefly— briefly only because suddenly Teddy and Charlie had flanked them, clambering to be part of the embrace. Ethan laughed aloud in pleasure, reaching down to hoist them up, kissing them each in turn and then moving in to kiss Sarah.

"Are you going to be my daddy now?" Teddy asked.

"Yes," Ethan replied, smiling, a smile that reached his eyes.

"Well, for goodness sake!" The little boy exclaimed. "What took you so long?"

And the entire room erupted into laughter.

About the Author

After 20 years as a Speech-Language Pathologist, 20 years as a wife and 17 years as a mother, I found myself serendipitously surprised by inspiration which manifested itself in the form of my first novel, *Forged in the Jungles of Burma*. Although I was always an avid reader, I never expected to write a book of my own, and yet here I am sharing with you my third novel. I find the time to write in between spending time with my husband and two children, working, camping, hiking, biking, canoeing, and, of course, reading.

D. C. Shaftoe lives in the Niagara Region of Ontario, Canada.

Acknowledgements

To my wonderful husband for his ongoing and everlasting support. I'm happy to be associated with you, darling.

To my children who go out of their way to support and help me.

To my family who buy my books, read my scenes and encourage me.

To Marty for helping me get my website started.

www.dcshaftoe.com

Coming Soon

Lethal Intentions:
The Battle for Gideon
Book One of the Second Chance Series

While you wait, check out www.dcshaftoe.com
Check out D C Shaftoe on Facebook.

Excerpt from Forged in the Jungles of Burma

<u>Prologue</u>
Soaring above the majestic mountains, the Boeing-747 carried Caroline closer to Singapore. *Finally, I can step forward into this second life, this second life I didn't ask for but was given nonetheless.* Three years after her first love died, Caroline embarked on a new life. She pulled out her airline tickets to remind herself: Pearson Airport in Toronto to London, England; one week to tour the museums and galleries; then on to Singapore. *Administrating a school for missionaries' children, who would have thought?*

Caroline gazed out the airplane window at the dark and light clouds pillowed below her. A bump and a growl interrupted her thoughts. The next bump sent her hands flying to the opposing ends of her seatbelt, fastening them snugly across her middle.

"This is your Captain speaking. We are currently experiencing mechanical difficulties. In the interest of safety, we will be landing at the Yangon International Airport in Myanmar. Please fasten your seatbelts. Thank you."

A ripple of exclamations oscillated through the cabin: "What's happening?"; "Where are we?"; "Myanmar? Is that Thailand or Burma?"

A barely heard, slightly exasperated growl of a whisper from her seat mate announced: "Myanmar is Burma, you ninnies."

Another bump sent Caroline's hands to grip her armrests. The airplane was now sinking through the clouds, the cumulonimbus electricity jolting the passengers. Beside Caroline, the Australian businessman, Dane Fowler, seemed oblivious to the discomfort of his fellow travelers, continuing to make notes on his laptop while the others murmured in dismay.

Circling once, the airplane shuddered onto the tarmac, grinding to a halt beside the old terminal, styled more like a

Buddhist temple than an airport terminal. The 747 dwarfed the several older regional carrier airplanes also parked nearby, while in the distance more familiar passenger airliners could be glimpsed parked in front of a more modern terminal.

Through the window, Caroline watched an animated discussion between the officious looking airport staff and the very agitated airline staff who, by their lively persuasion and perhaps a healthy bribe, finally won a limited liberty for the passengers. Disembarking, Caroline followed Dane's auburn head closely, seeing him as her only familiar contact in this alien land. The ornate carvings and figures which formed the golden edges of the roofline were echoed in the heavy golden doors which were constructed to appear carved.

The stewards led them in through these beautiful doors and over to a more austere area where sub-machine gun toting soldiers seemed randomly scattered around the rows of red plastic hard-backed chairs. While she could see some of the usual car rental desks in the distance, as well as several small souvenir or magazine stalls, this part of the airport, at least, had few amenities except what appeared to be some kind of restaurant off to the right of the area. This shoppe's entrance was graced by bright red columns bordering a forest green interior in which sat several people who looked like locals rather than tourists.

Taking all this in, Caroline remained intimidated by the sight of so many soldiers in one place, and stood uncertainly near the edge of this uninviting foyer, humming nervously and reminding herself that she wasn't in Canada anymore. Obviously very experienced world travelers, the unflappable Dane and his gold card invited Caroline and a few of the other wary and nervous passengers into the tea shoppe for a drink.

The little tea shoppe contained five or six tables, each with four chairs, and an L shaped red Formica-topped counter behind which the corpulent shoppe owner worked. Assorted foods were on display both on the counters and behind a glass partition. Caroline surveyed the assortment of fruits, the hot plates where various meats were simmering and the rice cooker steaming away. Dane handed over his credit card and indicated that the money would cover Caroline's drink as well as those of the other three passengers accompanying them. Caroline, not even coming close to understanding the language, ordered a milky tea by pointing at the picture on the menu. Dane ordered a deluxe tea boiled in condensed milk and the two of them adjourned to a small table at the front of the shoppe. The other three passengers sat at an empty table closer to the counter.

The burst of angry Burmese startled her and she turned to see two soldiers approaching a group of young women occupying a table in the darkest recess of the shoppe. One of the soldiers hauled a young woman from her seat, dragging her away from the table. Fear filled her expression as she thrust her arms against the man to free herself while, from under the table, a little girl rose, reaching for the woman's legs. Slapping the woman once, twice, three times, the soldier pushed her to the ground. As the other women rose from their chairs to help their companion, the tea shoppe owner yelled some sort of warning which drove them back to their seats.

One of the soldiers quickly wrapped his arms around the little girl and picked her up as she screamed and reached for her mother. The young mother's face fell in despair as she leapt to her feet, reaching for her daughter, all the while screaming at the soldiers who began to laugh at their little game. One of the soldiers grasped the front of her dress tearing it then following up with a punch to her stomach, yet still she struggled against him. The soldier's companion continued to hold the child firmly and it looked as if they meant to take her from her mother.

Glancing around desperately, Caroline waited for someone to intervene. Each pair of eyes she glimpsed was averted, each face unsympathetic. Caroline stood, eager to get help, but was pulled back to her seat by Dane's hand on her arm. As the assault continued, Caroline felt compelled to act. She couldn't stand by while men stole a child.

Standing quickly before Dane could grab her again, she strode over to the soldiers with no clear idea in her mind of what she was going to do. The shoppe owner grasped her shirt, gesticulating wildly and shouting at her in an incomprehensible language. Instinctively pulling away, her suddenly released hand sprang forward, slapping one of the soldiers in the face. Furious at his humiliation, he immediately produced a pair of plastic zip cuffs and securely bound her wrists while pushing her against the paneled wall. With her face planted against the paneling, she saw one of the young women slip out of the shoppe with the little girl while the soldiers were distracted.

Removed from the shoppe at gunpoint, Caroline, protesting, found herself bundled into an army jeep and led away to jail where she was placed in a holding cell crowded with the human equivalent of leftovers. Tried in court the next morning, she was subsequently brought here, to Bourey prison, never having seen a lawyer and never given the opportunity to contact the Canadian, or any other, embassy. As the cell door slammed shut, Caroline's confusion metamorphosed into terror.

Teaser Chapter from *Assassin's Trap*

Chapter One
Bombs, Plots and Terrorists
<u>Present Day</u>

Shards of glass scattered across John Brock's chest. Pain seared through his shoulder. *Blast!* He couldn't tell if his shoulder was broken or not. And he didn't take the time to check because through the shattered window, a groping hand grabbed for his keys…first a prybar, now the hand that wielded it.

Simultaneously wrestling with the disembodied hand, John swung his aluminum travel mug up and over his throbbing shoulder, ecstatic that he'd taken his coffee to go. The mug hit with a solid smack and John grinned in satisfaction at the grunt of pain in his right ear.

Not pausing to weigh the options, John slammed on his brakes. A body hurtled past and onto the asphalt. *Gotcha, you git!* Reversing, John spun the car 180 degrees, grinding the protesting gearshift straight to second as the staccato of automatic gunfire obliterated the rear window.

John wrenched the steering wheel sharply right, bouncing off the curb but continuing forward. He glanced in the rear-view mirror. A blue sedan pursued him. *Crap!* With the sedan behind and a fire engine blocking the street ahead, he was trapped. So when he noticed the narrow alley on his left, he turned into it.

Shifting his Volvo C30 to the left of the alley, John accelerated straight at a blue rubbish tip. At the last second, he cranked hard on the wheel, spinning and bouncing the car off the far wall of the alley. The airbag punched him in the face. Ears ringing, he still heard the blue sedan crash headlong into the tip.

First clearing his vision with a shake of his head, John tore his Glock from the glove box, disengaging the safety and chambering the first bullet. Holding his gun at the ready, he moved in slowly, scanning the seats in the vehicle. He saw only the driver slumped groaning over the steering wheel, a sub-machine gun held loosely in his right hand. John disarmed him easily, tossing the SMG beneath his own car.

"Raise your hands. Step out of the car," John said, adopting his best military voice, the voice which clearly conveyed the message that refusal was not an option.

"Hah!" A chuckle bubbled from the driver's frothy lips. "Y'all are dead, Brock," he said in a lazy Texas drawl. Then he raised his left hand slowly like a six year old playing cowboys. "Bang bang." The chuckle morphed into a bloody cough and John stepped back to avoid the crimson spray. *Yick!*

Wheezing in a breath, the Texan continued, "There's more a' comin'."

More? John's anger ratcheted up a notch. "Who are you working for?" The Texan sneered derisively and John repeated the question, the heat in his voice freezing to a deathly chill. "Who are you working for?"

But it was too late to find out. The blaggard was dead. *Blast!*

John checked through the car and searched the man's pockets to find...nothing. No identification. No clues. Nought of any use.

And then it started to rain. *Of course it's raining! It's London in winter.* John slapped his hands down on the roof of the blue sedan in an uncharacteristic release of temper. "Aargh!" Flipping open his mobile phone, he called his second-in-command.

"Horace Hibbert." The man's deep bass tones filtered through the phone and John could picture the affable giant running his fingers through his neatly trimmed afro.

"Hibb, I need your help. I'm in an alley just west of Aldersgate somewhere near St. Bart's Hospital. Are you still at Carter's campaign office?" John said.

"Things 'er fine down our end. It was a small bomb, not much damage," said Hibb.

"It's not that. I've been involved in an..." John paused, looking for a benign word to describe the situation. "Incident."

"Do you want me to send the plods over?" John could hear the concern in Hibb's voice.

"No, only you." John rang off. *There's more coming.* The threat replayed in John's mind as the rain poured down his already soaked body, the chill on his skin matching the chill in his heart.

When his mobile rang, he checked the caller ID. It was his wife. If he let the call go to voicemail, she might worry and, frankly, he could use a little *Caroline* about now.

Pausing to wipe the water from his phone, he answered, trying to keep his voice easy and light. "What's up?"

"Hi, sweetheart," Caroline said. "The Home Secretary called. He wants to meet with you when you're finished at the campaign office."

"Cheers," he replied.

"John. What's wrong?" But of course his wife would hear right through the attempted calm.

"Nought. The car's broken down but don't worry, Hibb is on his way to me."

"Darling, what happened?" He heard the edge that accompanied the concern in her voice. The last year, since John had begun going on operations again, they'd argued endlessly, it seemed, about disclosure; she wanted to know where he went and what he did on his operations and he refused to tell her, hiding behind the Official Secrets Act. John simply couldn't put Caroline at risk by revealing classified information which would likely only put her in danger or terrify her and send her running from him; information such as the fact that assassins had just attempted to terminate his existence using a prybar, a blue sedan and an SMG.

"John. What happened?" She sounded annoyed by his hesitation in responding.

"A spot of car trouble but I'm all right, I assure you. Do you think you could get a clean suit ready for me? I'll meet you on the third floor in the medical suites," he said.

"John." He could hear both the frustration in her voice and then the moment when she gave in. "Okay," she said. Her voice quavered but he couldn't tell which emotion set it to quake, anger or anxiety. "How long?" she asked.

"Not long. I'll need to drop the car over to the panel beater, I'm afraid," he said.

"The what?" she said. Normally, he would have chuckled at what his wife termed the English-Canadian-vocabulary-gap but there was no humour in him.

"Body shop," he clarified.

"Oh. That's fine. Are you sure you're alright?" she asked again.

Oh, just tickety-boo. "I'm fine. I'll see you shortly," he replied.

Within minutes, Hibb arrived, carrying an umbrella to cover them both. At his approach, John straightened, framing his emotions into a look of confidence and control.

"I take it this was no simple crash," Hibb said, gesturing at the Glock in John's hand.

Outstanding deduction! John swallowed his sarcasm, replying instead with a decisive, "Correct." Providing a rundown of the events to Hibb, he quickly moved on to a plan of action, "I need to get an ID on this fellow." *And then I need my wife.*

"How did he know where you'd be?" Hibb asked, clearly puzzled.

"Bomb in London. Political target. Not difficult to guess that I'd make my way here eventually." *If he somehow knew that I was the Head of Counter-Terrorism for MI-5.* "The plods and fire services have all other accesses blocked making this the most likely route," John said. It all sounded so reasonable until you realized that only a handful of people actually knew what John did for a living.

"John, do you think he…" Hibb nodded at the dead Texan. "Had summat to do with the bombing of Carter's campaign office? Could he have planted the bomb to draw you out?"

"Let's find out," John responded fiercely.

"You're looking ragged," Hibb observed, eyeing him up and down. "Need a lift to Casualty?" John shook his head and then froze at Hibb's next question. "What are you going to tell Caroline?"

Holding his Section Chief's gaze, John replied tonelessly, "That's not your concern." And then for some reason he couldn't fathom, he continued, "I told her I had a spot of car trouble."

"You really think she's going to be satisfied with that?" Hibb asked.

Why did I even answer? On most days, John was glad that Caroline had agreed to be his administrative assistant. She was a brilliant analyst, well-respected and liked by her colleagues, unfortunately to the point now where they had become quite protective of her. On other days, like today, John wished he could return to the time before Burma when he'd been the undisputed autocrat of his section; *Ironheart*, the ultimate spy, his emotionless life neatly compartmentalized.

"You're my officer not my counselor," John grumbled.

Hibb muttered something unintelligible in response, unintelligible but clearly spoken with intent.

John rose threateningly. "What did you say?" Heat flushed his cheeks.

Unperturbed, Hibb replied, "I said, that would be an underpaid job." And then opened his mobile to ring for a clean-up crew to collect evidence and sanitize the environment, returning it to backstreet London *normal*.

The 'Sanitation Unit' arrived and John briefed them on the evidence he wanted collected. Then he hitched a ride with

Hibb back to Thames House, headquarters of MI-5. Caroline met him on the third floor wearing black slacks and a cream-coloured blouse. John thought she looked both angry and concerned…and beautiful.

Her chestnut hair was swept into the new hairstyle she was trying out, a "fred" or a "wedge" or some such. Her round face held a softness. In fact, her entire body and her spirit held a softness he loved and his hands itched to touch her familiar curves. But the expression on her face held him in check. Even though she stood several inches below his six feet, she was nonetheless very intimidating with her hands on her hips. Her deep brown eyes looked annoyed but, always, always he could see her love for him written clearly within them.

"Car trouble?" Caroline asked and her skepticism was blatantly evident in her voice and manner. "John, what happened? You've got a cut over your eye. Your shirt's been shredded by…" She scanned his clothing, looking up to meet his gaze. "Broken glass?"

"An accident. The airbag deployed." He supplied the minimum required information, always hoping that she wouldn't ask for more.

He didn't miss her sigh as she stepped closer and slipped off his ruined blue silk tie and his suit jacket. Her warm fingers brushed his skin as she undid the buttons on his powder-blue shirt revealing the long welt across his chest and shoulder.

"That…was not caused by the airbag." Her fingertips gently traced the bruise and he was tempted to hum happily at the tender contact. "It looks like someone hit you with a baseball bat or an iron bar," she said. Really, she was much too clever to dupe so rather than argue or lie, he remained silent. She may suspect that he was attacked but if he didn't confirm it, she didn't need to feel the fear of danger. "John!" She clearly wanted to question him, interrogate him really. "Wha—"

And then he just didn't want to argue so he began to sing. "I like the sound of your sweet, gentle kiss…" He moved minutely closer to her. "The way your fingers run through my hair…"

"Boyzone. I Love The Way You Love Me," she said and the grim line of her mouth relaxed just a little.

"Please?" And he held his hands out palms-up in a gesture of surrender, begging her for comfort. "Please."

He watched her struggle for a moment more and then her arms were around him, her love erasing the fear and frustration from his chest.

"Never mind. I'm glad you're okay." She pulled his head to her shoulder. He slid his arms around her waist, sighing against her and kissing her neck. For a moment, he was fascinated by the trail of goose bumps his cold lips left behind.

"I love you, Caer," he murmured against her skin.

Shivering lightly, she stroked her fingers through his wet and sweaty hair. "I love you, too, my bear."

Pulling back, he let her remove his shirt. He waited patiently as she washed his cuts, applied a butterfly bandage above his eyebrow and kissed his bruises better. Everything felt better when Caroline took care of it.

"Why won't you tell me what happened?" Caroline asked. Her voice was soft and sad.

"It's nothing you need to worry about," John assured her. "I'm fine."

"You know," she said. "Just because you say that, doesn't mean I actually stop worrying."

Sighing morosely, he pleaded with her, "I don't want to argue. I hurt. I have a headache…" And he knew she saw the sorrow in his eyes because he didn't bother to hide it. And, because she really was incredible, she let him off the hook. He pulled her close, so relieved to have her in his arms, loving him. Loving him in spite of all it took to be married to Ironheart, the ultimate spy.

Soon after, bandaged and dry, John rode in the back of the service pool car on the way to Whitehall, the centre of Her Majesty's Government. As they wove their way along the Embankment, the grey clouds even parted for a moment revealing a rare glimpse of the sun's rays shining through the London Eye.

"Shall I wait for you, sir?" the driver said.

"Yes. I shan't be long," John replied, stepping out of the car. With a nod to Big Ben, England's famous clock tower, John walked past the wrought iron fence and on into the Cabinet Office to meet with the Home Secretary, Sir Desmond Stanway.

"Good afternoon, Mr. Brock," said Sir Desmond, simultaneously offering his hand in greeting and undoing the straining button on his suit jacket to make room for his hefty belly before he sat.

"Good afternoon, Home Secretary," John replied. He remained standing out of deference. "I have a preliminary report on the Carter bomb. The explosion occurred today at 5:45 am in the campaign office of Nigel Carter of Her Majesty's loyal opposition. Three casualties. No fatalities. Four groups have stepped forward claiming responsibility but none are credible."

"I want you to make this a priority. I've arranged with Commander Winters of the Met to coordinate your efforts with Counter-Terrorism Command. I'll expect you to offer your gratitude for his cooperation in person," Sir Desmond said.

Excuse me? "Of course, sir," John said. *How much manpower is necessary to investigate one simple bomb? And why am I expected to glad-hand the Met?*

"Very good," Sir Desmond said, gesturing for John to sit before he continued, "Before you leave, I have an urgent matter to discuss with you. The Chairman of the Joint Intelligence Committee passed this information on to me.

Apparently, MI-6 intercepted a communiqué which originated in Mumbai, India and terminated in Drammen, Norway. They believe the receiver to be one Tor Grendahl, a known—"

"Merc," John said. "A mercenary. A freelance hit man. What is the message and how does it concern MI-5?"

Silently, John took the sheet of paper the HS offered. It read, LOCATE: PET BADGER. VERY PRECIOUS. REWARD IF FOUND DEAD. And beneath the heading was John's own picture, taken in Moor Mead Garden from the looks of it, likely when he was walking their dog, Rufus.

Steeling his expression and releasing no emotion, John replied, "Thank you, sir. I'll look into it."

"I have spoken to Special Branch and been assured that they will organize protection for you and your wife," Sir Desmond said. "You live in Twickenham, do you not? They can have a security team in place within the hour. You are a fine officer, Mr. Brock. The Crown has no desire to lose your services."

"Thank you, sir, but I'll organize my own protection." *That way, Caroline will never have to know.*

The HS watched him silently for a moment and John could read his concern plainly in his eyes. "Very well, Mr. Brock. It is your prerogative."

John rose, shook the man's hand and departed, returning to the pool car. *This is why, against the culture of English security and law enforcement, I always have a handgun at the ready.* John sank into thought, not even noticing when the car stopped.

"We're here, sir," the driver said as they arrived at the Millbank entrance to Thames House.

John pulled himself mentally back to the present and exited the vehicle. He walked through the door with the tourists, making a left and then a right to the door marked "STAFF ONLY", swiping his security pass and entering the restricted zone. He mounted the few steps, paced along a corridor and then through the bulletproof security pods and onto the Grid, the office space for Section G, Counter-Terrorism.

Aubrey Davies met him with a statement that was likely meant to be a question.

"There's been some chatter from our assets in the Indian arms trade during the last forty-eight hours," Aubrey said. A long time veteran of the Security Services, Aubrey Davies' domain was the technology of espionage and counter-espionage. His brilliant intellect stood side by side with his social ineptitude cached within his fifty-five year old body complete with hunched shoulders and squinty grey eyes that were permanently lined from spending too much time chasing down ones and zeroes.

"And we're only hearing about this now?" John said.

"Shall I pass the information on to MI-6?" Aubrey said, reaching up to scratch along the edge of his receding hairline as though he sought to stop the glacial decline of his youth.

Something about Aubrey's manner warned John that his question had a deeper meaning. "Should I assume that you're not content with that course of action?" John asked.

"It seems to me that, given the dodgy source of the rumours and the information Caroline uncovered about the Jammu Kashmir Liberation Front, there may be a connection here that MI-6 might overlook," Aubrey said.

John released an internal 'ah'. "Very well. Keep a copy of the information and pass along the Indian rumours. Agreed?" John said, gauging Aubrey's reaction, knowing that he'd guessed right when the man released a satisfied smile. It was important to let his officers feel appreciated, something Caroline was seeking to teach him.

But rather than return to work, Aubrey remained, alternately tapping a pencil against his trouser leg and his lower lip.

Eyeing the graphite stains, John furrowed his brow to express his impatience with the man's stalling. "Out with it, Aubrey."

"Well," Aubrey began slowly. "I understand that Caroline's had her issues with the telephone system, but..."

Issues? John mused. That was an understatement. Caroline consistently disconnected the Home Secretary and, on more than one occasion, had set off the emergency shutdown protocol when she was meant to transfer calls.

Aubrey cleared his throat, continuing, "Er, Caroline...well, stone the crows! She has an uncanny ability to see to the heart of people and the issues surrounding them. We could make much better use of her talents as an intelligence analyst rather than an administrative assistant." John felt his gaze tighten and he noticed Aubrey hesitate before continuing. "Er, remember the Smythe case? None of us understood the significance of what she detected in his banking patterns. What about the ex-minister Sheldon? She sussed him out the first time she met him...and informed us all that the man was having an affair...which turned out to be the truth. And with the mistress of the ranking Russian officer in London who was a KGB agent."

"They're called the FSB now," John reminded Aubrey tersely for the umpteenth time.

"Nevertheless. She's very bright," Aubrey said. His voice was suddenly sure and definite.

John frowned, belying his next words. "I'm grateful, Aubrey. It's not really possible for me to promote my own wife." *And don't think for a moment that I would ever allow her to be involved operationally. She is much safer as she is, answering phones and typing reports.*

John's gaze drifted across the room to the desk where Caroline sat, mercifully oblivious to the danger of a hit man. John had made a long list of enemies in his time first with Special Forces' Maritime Terrorism Command and then with MI-5. His enemies were not the sort to cringe at the thought of using his wife as leverage against him. The very idea chilled his heart.

"I don't mean to waffle on about it…but, there! I may have a word with the DG," Aubrey said.

"Anything else?" John asked, eager to end this conversation before his wife overheard them talking about her. The last thing he needed was for Caroline to decide that she wanted a more active role in the defense of the realm. When Aubrey shook his head, John asked, "Have you seen Hibb?"

"Nipped down to Human Resources to get Ryan's new badge sorted," Aubrey said.

"He's lost it again?" John inquired, feeling the familiar thrust of annoyance that Ryan's ineptitude always seemed to elicit. He would never understand how the young man came to be recruited. If John hadn't been in Burma at the time, Ryan never would have been assigned as a field agent on his team. The young ginger-headed blighter was a liability.

"Indeed," Aubrey replied. "Hibb should return shortly." Aubrey retreated to his lair, the computer and technology laboratory of the Grid.

Crossing the Grid to Caroline's desk, John paused to watch her studying the computer screen before her, every measure of her body immersed in her task. Fear rolled through his belly. A contract on his life was nothing new, but he'd never before had something to lose; never before that one remarkable day in a dingy, terrifying prison in Burma, when he'd met Caroline…and loved her. Defying all the odds of his hard and lonely life, she'd loved him in return. She'd married him, taking his name, taking his life as her own.

For a moment, he gave in to the need to have her attention focused on him. "Could you please…" he began, leaning forward on his arms. Watching her eyes shift from the computer, he saw the furrow of concentration ease from her brow. And she smiled at him. She could smile with the greatest joy. As her gaze settled on him though, her smile reversed into a frown.

"What's wrong now?" she asked.

Her question took him by surprise. "Nought, sweetheart," he replied, but he knew that she didn't believe him because she narrowed her deep brown eyes in skepticism. How she could see through him was a mystery. He had earned the nickname, Ironheart, in part because he maintained complete control of his emotions and was adept at hiding them from others. But, somehow, she always knew.

"John." She interrupted his thoughts, warning in her voice. "I can tell there's something wrong. And don't give me that 'nought' crap because it won't fool me." And he thought he loved her more in that moment than ever before because she could always somehow find the 'real John Brock'. However, he did *not* want her to worry about him. After escaping with him through the jungles of Burma, she deserved a little tranquility. So he fobbed her off.

"Operational issues. Nothing for you to worry about," he replied. But she frowned at him and his heart sank within him. *Is it lying if I'm only keeping the information hidden for her own good?* Hoping to deflect her mood, he changed the subject and made his escape. "Could you please send Hibb in when he arrives?"

She nodded but the frown didn't shift. Covering a heavy sigh, he tucked his anxiety away. The truth was he never wanted to go back to life before Burma, before Caroline. He would never survive it.

Ten minutes later, Hibb knocked on his office door.

"Come," John said, inviting him into the glass-walled heart of the Grid.

Sitting behind his modern oak desk, John motioned for Hibb to shut the office door and take a seat, which he did, settling his gigantic frame into the straight-backed wooden chair across from John. Horace Reginald Hibbert, the name was as large as the man. An enigma to the majority of his colleagues, Hibb somehow managed to maintain a transparent Christian worldview amidst the shadowy translucency of espionage. John had quickly detected within Hibb the character of a good man, promoting him. Hibb fulfilled his role as Section Chief perfectly because everyone trusted Hibb.

"Bad news from the Home Sec?" Hibb asked. His voice was easy and light.

Without a word, John retrieved the folded sheet from his pocket and handed it over. Hibb seemed unfazed by the message, refolding it and raising his eyes to meet John's.

"Badger-Brock. That's twee," Hibb said. "This the third contract you've had on your life?"

"Fourth, actually, but that's not my concern," John replied.

"Is Special Branch providing security? I don't suppose you'll be moving into a safehouse or anything convenient like that?" Hibb asked.

And here was where things got tricky. John carefully kept his face void of emotion as he said, "I don't want Caroline to know."

"Aye?" Hibb's eyes widened in astonishment. "Why?"

"That's not your concern," John said. "I want this to stay between you and me and I want you to liaise with Special Branch to organize discreet security. You can put a couple of blokes on me if you like, but I want Caroline and the house covered. Understood?"

"Aye, sir. Wouldn't it be safer to simply tell her?" Hibb said.

"No. She's either with me at home or safe on the Grid," John said. *If I'm careful, she'll never know.*

"And when you're on assignment?" Hibb asked.

"I'll deal with that when it becomes necessary."

D C Shaftoe

ISBN 978-0-9684127-5-6

CPSIA information can be obtained at www.ICGtesting.com
Printed in the USA
LVOW07s2206250314

378972LV00011B/416/P